Borrowing Trouble

KADE BOEHME

KADE BOEHME

KADE BOEHME

ACKNOWLEDGEMENTS

First, I gotta thank Heidi for believing in me, even when I write stories that are totally not my norm.

I must thank, above all, Wendy, Meredith, Felice, and Nik for always being there to talk me off the ledge. Many times my neuroses would have stopped a book from getting titled, much less written without you angels to keep me sane.

And of course, none of this would matter without my absolutely amazing friends/family, my readers. This is all for you, babes.

DEDICATION

To the people who grew up with me HERE, where this book is based. It always felt like a land time forgot, and in so many ways it has. But I'm humbled and amazed at the few of you who still live there who've reached out to me as an adult. This one is to us, to our childhoods, to dirt roads and hayrides and lightning bug dreams.

To Montgomery County and the people who prove it's not the worst place to come from.

Borrowing Trouble

Chapter 1

Landon kicked his work boots on the doorstop before walking into the trailer that contained his father's office. His father was obsessive about muddy floors, a bit too obsessive for a man whose business was a saw mill. The whole mill was dirt and wood chips. Landon couldn't even walk across the driveway of Petty & Green Mills without tracking mud into his own truck and house every afternoon.

Once he was satisfied that his boots were as free of mud as they could get, he wandered in to where their office assistant, Ms. Lynne, sat on the phone bitching about something concerning insurance. As Landon handed over his trip report, he smiled fondly at the older woman who was rolling her eyes and making the *blah, blah, blah* hand gesture toward the phone. He felt for whoever was trying to tangle with Ms. Lynne, since she'd been doing this job for damn near twenty years. She was all of five-foot-five and constantly made up, her hair teased high, but one shouldn't be fooled by her southern grandma façade. She was all bulldog.

Landon walked to where they kept the coffee pot and poured himself a cup, trying to fend off the cold. "Landon," Ms. Lynne called out. He turned back to her. She held her hand over the mouthpiece of the phone and continued, "Your Daddy wants you to pop in the office before you head out on your next load."

"Yes, ma'am," he confirmed with a nod and headed to his dad's office, sipping his coffee. He was surprised his dad was even in his office. The old man was usually out supervising the hell out of everyone. His dad was a strict boss, but he was fair, and for their little county in Mississippi, he paid well.

The office door stood open, so Landon stuck his head in and knocked on the door frame. "Knock-knock. Ms. Lynne said you needed to see me."

Landon's dad looked up and waved his son in with a grunt. Ricky Petty was a burly man, three inches taller than Landon's five-feet-ten, and built like a barrel with a pair of sticks for legs. His grunt was one of his *good mood grunts*. Landon and his mother had turned deciphering his father's grunts into an art, though his father was not a complicated man. He was big and intimidating, with a red beard and dark brown hair always covered in a straw cowboy hat that shaded his dark brown eyes enough to make him seem much surlier than he was. He was actually just your typical country-bred, good ol' boy with a teddy bear disposition— unless he was in a snit. Then he was damn near horrifying to watch. Landon had stayed out of trouble as a kid, the wrath of his father's rare temper and the firm set of his face when disappointed had been enough to make even a bigger man feel two feet tall.

Landon plopped down in the wooden chair that faced his father's desk, waiting for his dad to finish up whatever he was doing with the papers he was shuffling. Landon had finished his coffee before his dad finally looked up. "Sorry, son. Lynne and I are dealing with new hire insurance horse puckey." Landon smiled at his dad. The old guy was not one for cursing, and Landon found his silly curse-word replacements endearing, coming from such a big man.

"You guys hired someone new?"

His dad grunted an affirmative, then shut the folder containing the papers he'd been fiddling with. "We finally hired on a new manager so you can focus on hauling full time."

Landon breathed a sigh of relief. He'd been hauling full time as well as handling overseeing the day-to-day management of the mill, so he was usually around until late in the night dealing with schedules and payroll. His dad had been looking for a while for someone so Landon could focus on the part of the job he liked most, hauling their wood chips from the mill down to the plywood and paper plant in Laurel, Mississippi. It was typically a six hour round trip, and when you started at three in the morning and didn't get home 'til eight at night, it made for a long day. Plus, his dad really wanted someone around to help on-site so they could both cut out earlier than they had been over the last year since his dad had bought out his partner, Jimmy Green.

"That's great, Dad. Decided not to use one of the old timers?"

"Naw. They all sniffed around the job but wanted the extra pay without the extra hours."

Not surprising at all. He wasn't sure how good they'd take to an outsider coming in as their boss, but his dad knew best. And Landon had no interest in being manager anymore, so he'd take what he could get.

"Marty Bennett told me his son-in-law was looking for better paying work."

Landon furrowed his brow, trying to remember the son-in-law in question. "Bethany's old man? Thought she was in Atlanta?"

"Name's Jay. I s'pose they're actually split up. She's off at Emory. Marty says he's a good guy, though. Let her go off and get some fancy degree and keeps the kids during the school year. Marty figures they'll end up back together at some point, high school sweethearts and all."

Landon smiled again. "You old men are as bad as the blue haired ladies with your gossipping."

His dad harrumphed. "Nothin' wrong with a man wanting his kid happy. Thinks they're a good fit and Jay's a good family man, treats his girl well. It's best for those kids, you know." Landon's dad and his friends were old school, so they would think that. Landon thought he remembered Jay from the couple times the man stopped by when Bethany had babysat Landon. They were both a good seven or so years older than him, so he didn't remember either of them all that well.

"When's he start?" Landon asked.

"Monday, next week. You should come by tomorrow and meet him. Your mama is makin' dinner for him and his kids over at the house tomorrow night."

"You know I wouldn't miss a free meal, pops." Landon also wanted to meet the man he'd undoubtedly have to train before they got mired in the work.

"Your mama will be happy to hear it. You can cut out early since it's Friday, so come on over to the house at six o'clock."

"Will do. Anything else you need?"

"That's all. You get on out on the road again. We'll be seeing you tomorrow."

"Yessir," Landon confirmed, and headed on out to check that his next trailer was loaded. He couldn't wait to shake the man's hand who'd be lightening his work load. Hopefully, he wouldn't have too many days left like this one where he'd have to come in and write up payroll. Maybe he'd actually be able to get out to Jackson on the weekends and scratch a long-burning itch he'd let fall by the wayside for months now.

***

Landon showed up at his parents' house the next night a little after six. He'd managed to get all the payroll checks passed out and still had time for a shower and a change of clothes. Thank God for small favors, he wouldn't meet his new mill manager in dusty, day-old clothes and muddy boots. Not that the man would actually be paying attention, and he'd sure understand if Landon was dirty, since he presumed the man was used to dirty work clothes.

Landon had seen the man's application and his work experience was full of welding, mechanical, and mill work. Hired as a favor to a friend or not, the man had almost twenty years of solid hands-on experience, so he was more than qualified for the position he was stepping into. He'd even been a supervisor at the steel plant he'd worked at in Tupelo before moving back to his hometown. Ms. Lynne knew the family and had shared that Jay had moved to get his kids closer to his in-laws so they'd have family around while he worked.

Landon parked his truck in his parents' massive, dusty yard next to his father's dually and pet their two black labs that ran out to him as his mother opened the front door. "There's my handsome son!" She waved from the porch as Landon approached.

Hugging her neck, he greeted, "Hey, Mama."

"Glad you could make it for dinner. You work too hard, I never get to see you anymore."

"Hopefully this new manager is gonna change that."

"He's a nice man. Your daddy seems to like him."

"That's good," Landon said with a smile, walking in the house and shedding his jacket. His mother took his jacket and hung it up on her overstuffed coat rack by the door. She asked him about work as he followed her to the kitchen-slash-dining room. As they approached, he could hear his father's booming laugh, which meant his dad must really like the guy.

"Jay, do you remember my son, Landon?" his mother asked when they turned the corner into the room. Landon blinked and willed his body to behave when he took in the form of the new manager he was going to be training. *Holy hell.*

The man was as tall as Landon's father, slimmer in the mid-section, but well-muscled up top from hard work. The baby blue henley he was wearing was tight on his chest and biceps, which were nicely defined. The lighter blue of the shirt set off his sun bronzed skin. His short brown hair and stubbled beard had a few lighter patches that'll probably grey in another five years or so, but he didn't seem all that much older than Landon. Those light patches only served to make him more attractive. Kind brown eyes crinkled at the sides with a smile that nearly took Landon's knees from under him. Jay extended a large hand at Landon, who stood blinking for just long enough that his mother had to smack his shoulder.

Landon shook his head to snap himself out of his embarrassing daze and walked forward to shake the man's hand. "Surely this can't be little Landon? Last time I saw you, you couldn't have been more than ninety pounds dripping wet."

I'm not twelve years old anymore, man. And his cock was sure reminding him he was well past puberty the way it started perking up at just the contact of their hands. "Uh, yeah. Been a while. Sorry, I don't remember you much."

And that was a total lie. Landon remembered now being thirteen the last time he'd seen Jay Hill. Jay'd been twenty, and he was at a Christmas party with Bethany and their baby son. Landon's body reacted much the same as it was today. He couldn't believe he'd forgotten how incredibly attractive Jay was, and damn if they man hadn't gotten better with age. It was going to be torture working every day with this guy.

Thank goodness I won't be at the mill as much.

But the glaring reminder that the man was straight made itself known as he turned to introduce his now sixteen-year-old son, Clint, and his twelve-year-old daughter, Millie. They both looked like their father, which was lucky for them because his genes had produced handsome children.

"Landon here's gonna be training you," Landon's father beamed. "He's been managing the mill while we looked for a new manager." He patted Landon on the shoulder proudly. "He's been a big help while we've been short-handed."

Jay's eyes went wide. "You've been managing and makin' hauls?" Jay seemed impressed.

"Yeah, it's been a long year. Glad to have someone to take some of the load." Landon almost groaned when his brain immediately supplied a dirty connotation to his latter statement. Oh, this was gonna suck. And not in a good way.

"I'm just glad for the work. Hope I don't disappoint."

Landon's father waved off Jay's concern and assured the man he was sure they'd made the right decision bringing him on.

Regardless of his traitorous dick, Landon couldn't help being relieved. His dad was usually a good judge of this stuff and Landon felt that much closer to being free of so much extra responsibility. He also reminded himself how long it'd been since he'd gotten laid. He would be able to go to Jackson, to the bar, and find someone for some fun once he got Jay trained up. That'd surely make the whole horny-for-the-straight-man thing easier to handle.

He hoped.

Chapter 2

Jay hugged his daughter and told her goodnight before wandering to Clint's room. He knocked and stuck his head in. "Hey, Clint."

Clint looked up from his laptop with a smile. "What's up, Dad? Have a good time?"

Jay tried his best to contain the grimace that tried to steal over his face. "Was your sister good for you?" he deflected.

"Yeah. Expected you to be later, honestly." Clint rolled his eyes when Jay harrumphed.

"No, I gotta work early tomorrow. Thanks for watching Millie."

"No problem. Glad you got out for a while. It's been too long."

"Yeah, well." Jay didn't want to touch that, but he felt lucky to have such great kids. They'd taken his first foray into dating life in stride. They'd had three years to get used to the idea, but he still felt weird telling them where he was going tonight. "Thanks anyways. Lights out in thirty, okay?"

Clint nodded his assent and went back to whatever he

was doing on his laptop. His kids were great. They could have been much harder on him for moving them back down to Webster county or making them switch schools, but after three years, he'd needed a little more help than he could get in Columbus and his ex's parents had mentioned that the Pettys had an opening for a manager at their mill. The new job meant more time at home. The pay wasn't quite as much, but it was comparable, and the cost of living was half what he'd been paying. The kids were glad to have more dad time and to see their grandparents. Since Jay's parents were dead and their mother was in Atlanta, they'd missed having family around so it hadn't been a hard sell. Yeah, they'd balked at moving to the sticks at first, but it had gone much more smoothly than Jay had expected.

Jay made his way downstairs to the kitchen and grabbed a beer and his cell phone before stepping on the back porch. As he dialed his ex-wife, he breathed in the fresh air and enjoyed the silence that came with not having neighbors for miles. He'd missed having a whole corner of the earth to himself.

"Jay!" Bethany's happy voice chirped through the earpiece of his phone.

"Hey, Beths. Kids said you called. Sorry to return it so late."

"How'd your date go?" He fell silent, surprised she'd asked, because he hadn't mentioned the date. He should have known one of the kids might, though. He couldn't tell if Bethany was happy he'd started seeing other people or not, though like Clint, she thought it was about time after three years.

His only response was to groan good naturedly, attempting to keep the mood light.

Bethany laughed her familiar, tinkling laugh that made Jay smile. He was happy they'd stayed close. Their divorce had been extremely amicable, she'd been his best friend practically his whole life, after all.

"She spent the whole night trying to talk me into bringing the kids to her church."

Now it was Bethany's turn to groan. They'd been a fairly liberal couple for being born-and-bred country kids from Montgomery County, Mississippi. But the town—or unincorporated community if you wanted to be all official—they'd grown up in didn't even appear on a map and shared both a zip code and phone prefix with a nearby one-stop-sign town. With a population of just a little over four-hundred, their hometown still boasted around eight rural protestant churches, and more than thirty in the county itself, so it'd been part of every resident's Sunday growing up. So the fact that Jay and Beth had moved to a larger town and had not forced their kids into Sunday school, vacation bible school, and at least one youth group, had been a bone of contention with Bethany's parents.

"She even said she could 'look past' the divorce issue."

"Oh, good lord. Where'd you find this woman?"

"You know Stewart," he sighed, referring to their hometown. "Near as soon as I moved in, they asked when we'd work our issues out. And when I said there were no issues to work out, they started pushing girls from their churches on me."

"Good grief. Good to know some things never change."

"No kidding."

"I had a date tonight too, but that was about as unsuccessful. When I said I was from Mississippi, he acted like he was surprised I knew how to use silverware and wear shoes."

Jay snorted. "Nice."

"How's the new job?"

Jay had no complaints there. Over the last three weeks, he'd grown to enjoy his new job. The work was hard, but that was nothing new to him. He didn't like how much time he spent over a desk doing bullshit payroll and logging mileage, but the boss seemed to like him and Landon was a competent trainer. He was still impressed that a man as young as Landon was so responsible, seeing how he had taken care of things for his dad at the expense of his own time and social life. The guy had admitted to not getting out much himself.

"It's good. Ricky's a good man to work for. The crew works hard and has been pretty accepting of me as their new boss since I'm a local boy. Most of 'em know your dad, so I'm sure that helps."

"That's real good. I talked to the kids. They said they're

liking school."

"They've been great. They can't wait to see you, though."

"Oh right, I meant to tell you, my fall break is the same week as theirs, so if you don't mind them coming up that week, I'd love to have them."

"Of course." Jay loved his kids, but a week to kick back at home with just himself and the crickets would be nice. Since the kids came back from staying with Bethany for the summer, it had been chaos between moving, the new job, and typical teenage dramas. They missed their mom as much as he missed his best friend, but he knew they'd made the best decision.

"Great, well, I ought to get off the phone. I have work early. You have a good night, Jay. Sorry your date didn't go well."

"Sorry about yours too, Beths. Have a good night."

When they hung up, he stayed on the back porch, finishing off his beer. He was glad he and Bethany had appeared to have made the right decisions. At least, he felt like they had. He knew the original reason for the kids to stay with him during the school year was because they were supposed to keep things status-quo, but over time and with Bethany's new job, he knew she missed them terribly, but everything continued to fall in place as it should and they all seemed to be moving on well. He couldn't help but wonder if the other shoe might drop. Seemed things had always gone a little too well. The only thing that had been awkward was when people were shitty to Bethany for leaving her kids "just to go to school."

Jay didn't begrudge her the need to go back. They'd married so young, fresh from high school, because that was what you did. With time and maturity, they'd grown to be great friends but no longer lovers, and the need to make their ways in the world beyond what they'd been expected to do had grown to be a heavy weight on their marriage. It had hurt at first for everyone, but they were all settled now after all these years and the kids seemed to be doing well, so they hadn't done any irreparable damage.

He hoped.

****

"Ugh. That's why I don't let them set me up," Landon teased. "They mean well, but my God, the church invitations get so fuckin' old." Landon had overheard Jay telling Ms. Lynne about his abysmal date.

"I told them thanks for tryin', but I'm gonna find my own dates from here on out." Jay only half meant it. He didn't really have much interest in trying to date any more than he'd done. It was awkward. He didn't miss his ex that way, at all. He missed the companionship and sure, he missed sex, it'd been almost six months without it before Bethany announced she might go back to school. Almost four years with his hand was definitely a hardship, but he'd had enough to focus on that the only time it sucked was when he went to bed alone, yet again, when the kids were gone.

"Well, I better head on out. Looks like my trailer is ready to go," Landon announced. They'd been friendly as one could expect, but Jay thought Landon always seemed to avoid much personal conversation and seemed to try not to spend more time than necessary in Jay's company. It sucked, really, because out of all the people he'd reconnected with since he'd come back home, Landon seemed like the person he had the most in common with. When the man wasn't being too guarded, he was pretty funny.

And for the life of Jay, he couldn't figure out why he gave a damn if the man was guarded. That sounded like something Bethany said about him to the marriage counselor when they talked about the last few years of their marriage at therapy. Now he was off worrying about someone else's inability to communicate.

While Landon trained Jay, they'd discovered they both liked the same football team and had a similar sense of humor. Landon also seemed oddly alone for a guy surrounded by people he'd known his whole life. Jay wasn't sure how he knew that, but it was a vibe he got. And Jay could sympathize. He'd never really fit in around home, Bethany having been his best and only friend before they'd gotten married and moved off. Somehow, though, he sensed a kindred spirit in Landon and it'd be nice to be in the company of an adult. He was getting tired of drinking beer on his back porch alone. The novelty was beginning to wear off.

"Hey, Landon, what're you up to this Saturday?" Jay wasn't sure what exactly made him want to invite Landon to hang out with him, especially since the man seemed not to want to fraternize, but damn if he wanted to spend his first kid free weekend in a while alone. And yeah, Landon was younger and probably had little interest in hanging out with someone almost ten years older than him, but Jay couldn't stop himself.

Landon raised an eyebrow and shrugged. "Nothin', I don't suspect. Was gonna go down to Jackson, but my friends backed out and I don't wanna go by myself."

Jay wondered what Landon did in Jackson. The city was bigger than their little town and probably offered better entertainment than anything a twenty-eight year old could get into here, but Landon never recounted tales of his times, even though he drove three hours just to go out. The other guys drove a little over an hour to go out and always came in on Mondays with tales of their weekends in the little honky tonk they frequented, so you'd think Landon would have tales to share of, what would have to be, more interesting bars. Or maybe Jay was being presumptuous in assuming Landon drove down to go to bars.

"I was thinking about catching the Ole Miss game at Woody's over in Winona," Jay offered. Landon's blue eyes blinked owlishly. He seemed to make that face a lot. Jay never could read the expression and it always made him feel like maybe he'd done something wrong. "It's no big deal. The kids are out of town at their mom's come Friday, so I thought I'd get out of the house."

Landon was silent for another moment before nodding, his expression giving away nothing. Finally, he shrugged one shoulder and an easy smile tugged up one side of his face, and Jay felt a funny feeling he couldn't put a finger on. "Sure. Better than getting drunk by myself."

Well, wasn't that heart-warming. "Glad you can be bothered."

"Oh, that's not what I meant." Landon held his hands up, neck flushing in the adorable way it did when he was flustered or embarrassed. *Adorable*? Jay was pretty sure that thought made him blink in a similarly owlish fashion. *What the hell?*

"Sorry," Landon apologized. "I'd like that. Haven't been to Woody's in a good minute."

"Uh, yeah." Jay looked down at his desk and shuffled papers, trying to cover his reaction to thinking another man was adorable. When Jay looked back up, he noticed Landon was looking like maybe Jay'd lost his mind.

"You okay?" Landon asked warily.

"Yeah. Sorry." Jay cleared his throat and fussed at himself to get it together. "State game starts at 7:15."

Landon gave a nod. "A'ight. See ya then."

Jay watched Landon leave, then caught Ms. Lynne's speculative gaze. He didn't like the narrowed eyes as they studied him. The last five minutes had been possibly the weirdest of his life.

"Real nice of you to invite Landon. He don't get out much," Ms. Lynne said with a feigned nonchalance.

Jay shrugged. "Seems to get out plenty to me."

"I s'pose," was all she had to offer. He didn't have anything to say to that either.

KADE BOEHME

Chapter 3

To say Landon was surprised by Jay's invitation to Woody's would have been an understatement. He was afraid he'd come off as an asshole over the last few weeks since he'd tried hard to stay away from the man. He'd done his damnedest to reign in his body's reaction to Jay Hill, but damn if the man wasn't like a flame to Landon's moth.

There wasn't much about Jay Landon didn't like. Physically, Jay was amazing, but as a man, Jay was even better. He worked hard, had Landon's father's respect, was a wonderful father, to hear most people tell it. But the man was straight. He had kids. He also had an ex-wife that he was still close with, who people thought he would get back together with.

Landon almost said no when Jay invited him out, but the man had seemed to genuinely want a friend to hang out with, though Landon couldn't figure out why Jay had thought of *him*. What could it hurt, though? Aside from his two best friends he only got to see sparingly, Landon didn't exactly have a burgeoning social life. His social life lacked even more when he stuck around his hometown for a while. What would one football game hurt?

He could put aside his lusty bullshit and ease two people's need for friendship by being a fucking adult and

20

going for a beer and football. That seemed much more fulfilling than another weekend of bitchy twinks at the gay bar he frequented in Jackson anyways. He was too damned old and lived a totally different life than the other twenty-somethings he met there.

Landon noticed Jay immediately after walking into Woody's. Woody's was an institution locally. A country grill and bar where you ate catfish and threw peanut hulls on the floor seemed to sum up the local color quite well.

"What's up?" Landon asked as he plopped down in the booth with Jay.

Jay smiled his kind smile and Landon was glad he'd decided to take the man up on his offer. He really was a nice guy. He couldn't imagine how shitty it must be to be surrounded by all the guys who didn't exactly want to party with the boss man, no matter how well they knew him. Landon welcomed that social divide, while Jay was probably suffering because of it since he seemed to spend all his time working or with his kids.

"Not much, man." Jay pulled a bottle of Bud Light from the bucket of beer he'd ordered and offered it to Landon. Landon accepted it with a thanks. "Just in time. I ordered some wings and cheese sticks just now."

"Perfect." Landon was famished. Even his first pull of the beer had him feeling buzzy, so he needed some food pronto. "Thanks for inviting me. I really was lookin' at another night of staring at four walls."

"Not much to do around here."

Landon snorted. *You have no idea.* "My friends live in Jackson now, but our schedules don't exactly line up all the time. Plus, it gets expensive fueling up my truck for a trip down once a week."

"I imagine so. What do y'all get up to down there?" Jay asked the question innocently enough, Landon would feel like an asshole not to answer. But he couldn't exactly say *"oh I go get my dick sucked by college boys so I don't horn up every time I'm around you."*

"Oh, not much. Hit the bars. More interesting people than Buddy's. I'm sure you've noticed the guys don't exactly want us to hang out with 'em anyways, so me showing up in Grenada wouldn't thrill 'em."

Jay smiled sympathetically. "Older crowd there. Hell, that crowd is too old for me."

"You're right about that."

"Anyways, thank you for coming out tonight. Too many nights being dad. Nice to get out for a beer with a buddy. Been a while."

"I bet. Must be hard, just you."

"Nah. It's not so bad. Beths and I have a pretty good set-up, and her parents help out a lot now that I'm back home."

Landon wasn't sure what made him say it, but he suddenly had the urge. "Sorry to hear about you and Bethany splitting up. Good y'all are still friends, though."

Jay shrugged again. "It just made sense. It wasn't a bad break up. Just grew up and grew apart."

"Well, it's nice of you to let her go off to school like you did."

"Nothin' nice about it. It was the right thing. She's gonna be able to provide a better life for herself and the kids. She's got a damn good job now. After she's done with her first year, she'll come back to be with the kids again."

There. Settled. She'd come back and it'd be just like the oldtimers said, Jay and Bethany would get back together. Nothing could make Landon kill his silly crush on the damn straight man like cold, hard reality. Not that there had been a chance before, anyhow.

"Okay, well that's a heavy subject."

"Oh. Sorry, man. Just been meaning to mention it since you came back, but didn't think it'd be right to bring it up at the office."

"No, it's alright," Jay said, offering another of his kind smiles. The cold water that had been dumped on his crush made the effect of that smile not burn as brightly as it had earlier. *Good. A friend.* Another he couldn't be out to, but a friend nonetheless.

"Oh look. Game's on." Jay pointed to the TV.

After a few more beers and some wings, they'd both relaxed and had a decent conversation. They'd talked about their days at the local high school, Jay's kids, and things as trivial as good places for hunting. Landon found himself having a great time. Jay was easy to talk to and didn't seem to have the good ol' boy attitude Landon expected from the man at first. Jay had talked about how they'd not forced the kids into church and how he and Bethany had spent a lot of time with a gay couple who lived on their street. That made Landon squirm a little, but it also made him think he might like having Jay around.

They ordered another bucket of beer and Landon excused himself to go to the bathroom. "Gotta break the seal." When he came back to the table, he was annoyed to find one of the women from the bar had eased over during his absence to squeeze onto the booth seat next to Jay. When he sat back down, Jay shot him an apologetic look, which was incredibly endearing.

"Heya, Landon." Jay sounded tipsy and his face was wide and happy when Landon sat back down. "This is Felicia."

"Landon and I are old friends," Felicia cooed, practically ignoring that Landon had returned. They were indeed old friends. She was only a year older than him and was a notorious bar fly. She'd slept with a few of Landon's friends and seeing her on Jay didn't surprise him in the least. Although, he had to give it to her, she had good taste, seeing as she was setting her sights on his new friend.

Landon didn't respond because it wasn't necessary, judging by the way Felicia was whispering in Jay's ear. He rolled his eyes, but couldn't help smiling at the goofy look on Jay's face. Too bad Landon couldn't get that response out of the man. But good for Jay. Someone deserved to get laid and, from the sound of things, it had been a while for Jay. And that moment served as yet another bright, blinking, neon reminder that Jay was very straight.

"Well," Landon said with a stretch. "I'm actually pretty whooped, Jay." Landon pulled his wallet out and dropped a couple twenties on the table before standing. "Think I'll head out."

Jay jerked his head away from Felicia and frowned. "Wait. Don't leave. The game's not even over." Felicia did not look pleased.

"Naw, don't worry about it. I'm just tired as hell. May as well head on back to the house." Landon wasn't exactly lying. He was tired as hell. It'd been a long week and he'd gone and helped his daddy work on his tractor early that morning. Felicia almost looked like she'd thank Landon for leaving if it wouldn't be entirely tacky. "Good to see you, Felicia." She waved dismissively as Landon left.

Landon made it to his truck before he heard his name being called. He turned to see Jay sauntering toward him. "You left your phone."

"Oh, thanks," Landon said, taking the proffered device. "Sorry 'bout that."

"Don't worry about it." Jay definitely sounded toasted, his speech a little slurred.

"You alright, big guy?"

"I don't think so. It's been a while since I drank away from the house. Or more than a couple beers, for that matter." Judging by how tipsy he was, a while probably measured in years rather than months.

"I'm sure Felicia's gon' take real good care of you, hoss," Landon teased. Hoss? *You hang around the saw mill too much.*

Jay frowned and looked down at himself. "I think Little Jay is too drunk to have any fun tonight."

Landon laughed. "That sucks. You need a ride?" It did suck. Landon had been there a few times. The mind was willing, but the body wanted no part of it.

"Fuckin' whiskey dick," Jay bitched. "Yeah, I prob'ly oughtta get a ride." And judging by the stumble to the side, Landon had to agree. Felicia suddenly appeared behind them.

"Y'all alright?"

"Felicia, I think my boy's had too much to drink."

Jay nodded sullenly.

"That's alright," she said. "I can give him a ride home."

Landon looked at Jay. "You want her to give you a ride?"

She wrapped a hand around Jay's bicep, pulling her keys from her purse. "Maybe you'll sober up and we can hang out for a while."

Jay looked uncertain, so Landon swallowed the tiny, eeny-weeny bit of jealousy that still remained and encouraged Jay to let Felicia take him. He didn't know bro-code etiquette on this situation. It'd seem like you'd help your friend get laid, but in this state, maybe not.

"No. Thanks anyway, Fiona." Jay gave her a too-bright, dimpled smile, obviously not realizing how pissed off Felicia looked. The *no* had already made her purse her lips, but forgetting her name had made her go red in the face. Landon covered his mouth so she couldn't see the smile.

Felicia snapped a *whatever* and went back inside. "Did you settle up the tab?" Landon asked around his chuckling.

"Wassfunny?" Jay honestly had no clue what faux-paz he'd made, and that made Landon laugh harder.

"Nothin', man. Just, get in my truck. Lemme go check that you paid out." He watched to make sure that Jay stumbled into the right truck, then went to check that the bill had been settled. He apologized to Felicia, who was very understanding when he mentioned Jay didn't go out much since he usually had the kids. She gave him a napkin with her number.

Landon tossed the napkin at Jay when he hopped into the cab of his F-250. "Here. My job as a wing-man has been fulfilled."

Jay took the napkin and blinked hard to focus on it. Landon could only shake his head and chuckle. After he dropped Jay off with a promise to come around in the morning to take him to his truck, Landon noticed the napkin was crumpled on the seat next to him. He couldn't help but be happy about that, though he didn't imagine it was more than a drunken mistake.

Chapter 4

Jay was embarrassed he'd gotten so damn drunk at Woody's. He'd apologized to Landon as soon as he saw him. He was accustomed to the occasional beer, but he'd overdone it without realizing it. He'd had a couple before he ordered the bucket and felt like a total jackass that he'd had to have a DD. Hell, his DD was the younger guy. Landon should have been the one that needed a ride, not Jay's almost-middle-aged ass.

Landon insisted it was okay, though. Jay'd had a good time hanging out with Landon, but he was mortified he'd embarrassed himself in front of the man. And he'd drunkenly admitted to Landon and a very attractive younger woman that his cock was out of the game because of a few beers. Jesus, he'd never get laid again at this rate. No doubt, after blowing off Fiona—Alicia? Felicia?—his ability to pull with even the sure-things was going to go out the window.

Jay was certain Landon wouldn't want to have a beer with him again since he couldn't hold his damn booze. Jay was surprised, though, when he offered to make it up to Landon and invited him over for football at his place and Landon accepted. Landon teased him every time he offered him a beer, but over the next three weeks, Landon had come over a couple times, sometimes just to shoot the shit.

It'd been nice having someone around while his kids were at his ex in-laws. The visits weren't much to write home about, but they would companionably chat about work or watch a game. The company was nice, but … that didn't account for the still indescribable contentedness he had in Landon's company. He'd had it once or twice with guy friends in high school, a co-worker in his earlier twenties, but he hadn't been close to many folks after the kids got older and life got more demanding.

He'd lost himself in his marriage at some point. Bethany had too. They freely admitted it to each other the day she came to him with the idea to finally separate. They were not much more than roommates. And life'd been good, simple, but he wasn't sure when he'd started feeling so old. He hadn't realized he had no one other than his kids and Bethany until he'd actually been on his own again.

That was what he figured these feelings were with Landon, like he finally had a friend again. A guy to pal around with. Someone who wasn't around to judge or talk about bills or expect anything from him. He loved his kids, and his family had always been important to him, but there was an easy peace that came with being around Landon.

"Hey, man," Landon said with a wave as he plopped in a chair next to Jay's desk, pulling Jay out of his thoughts.

"Hey. What's up, man?" Jay leaned back in his chair and stretched a bit.

"Wanna come to my house this weekend? We're doing a catfish fry—me, Mitchell, Brittany, and my folks.

It's kinda tradition the weekend before Thanksgiving. You can bring the kids."

Jay hadn't met Landon's two closest friends yet, but he'd heard plenty about them. "Bethany is coming down from Atlanta and taking the kids this weekend. They're spending the weekend with her parents, then off to hang out in the big city with their mama for Fall Break. So it'll just be me rattling around the house."

"Oh, yeah. Forgot you mentioned that. Well, definitely stop by then, if you feel up to it."

"Great, I'll plan on it."

"Awesome." Landon stood and went to drop his mileage log sheets on Ms. Lynne's desk. "Y'all have a good afternoon. I'm taking an extra load out tonight."

"Have a good afternoon, sugar," Ms. Lynne said with a pleasant smile.

Jay went back to his work, but didn't get far into it before Ms. Lynne sat in the chair Landon had just vacated. "Somethin' I can do for you, Ms. Lynne?"

"You and Landon sure seem to have gotten close."

Jay frowned at how she seemed to be accusing him of something, though of what, he wasn't sure. "Yes, ma'am."

She leaned in, conspiratorially. "Friendly word of advice."

Jay put down the pen he'd been writing with and crossed his arms over his chest, leaning back in his chair. "What's that?"

"Be careful. You're an attractive man, don't wanna give him no wrong ideas, is all."

Jay frowned. What the fuck did she mean by that? Ms. Lynne seemed fond of Landon, had worked with him for years. He didn't understand the disapproval that came off her in waves. "I don't think I get what you mean?"

"Look, I don't like to tell people's business. And I love that boy, known him since he was a little guy." She looked around as if someone might be listening around the corner. "Landon is a bit fruity, if you know what I mean."

Jay clenched his jaw. Yeah, he knew what she meant and it was fucked up of her to talk shit about Landon when he wasn't here to defend himself. What if she'd said these lies to someone who'd take it out on Landon's ass physically; someone who wasn't Landon's friend? "Ms. Lynne, I'm surprised at you."

"Now, don't look at me like that, Jay Hill. I don't never gossip and you know that." He did know that. She was loud and rough around the edges, but she was never one to talk out of turn. That was why this whole thing was surprising to him. "I just know you have him around your kids. I don't mind what a grown man chooses to do on his own time, but you know how they are…"

"Ms. Lynne." Jay's voice was full of warning.

"I'm just sayin'. 'Bout the only people who don't know it are his parents. Everybody knows when he goes down to Jackson, he's goin' to that gay bar. My nephew Tim seen it with his own eyes."

"So that means Tim was at a gay bar too?"

Ms. Lynne scoffed. "Means no such thing. There's a liquor store right by that bar and Tim was comin' out and happened to see 'im."

Jay was annoyed. Suuuure, Tim had been at the *liquor store*. *My left nut.* But could Landon really be gay? Not that he'd have a problem with it. Would he? It'd sure explain why Landon never seemed interested in any of the girls who tried to catch his eye when they were at Woody's. Did it really matter either way?

Jay was inexplicably more disturbed by the thought that Landon didn't trust him with that information then by the fact he was gay. Jay'd told Landon about his divorce and how hard it had been adjusting. He'd told Landon about how bad it'd hurt when he and Bethany lost the baby that had been the catalyst for their getting married in the first place. He knew being gay was a hard thing to admit to, especially where they lived. Surely, Landon would know Jay wouldn't judge him and neither would his kids. At least Jay liked to think none of them would. He hated to admit he'd never really thought anything on gays or gay rights. Didn't seem like something that was part of their world, though he knew that was silly.

Gays just seemed like a TV thing, a network news

thing, a city thing. Jay had never even met someone who was openly gay. Thinking Landon might be, he cringed to admit, boggled his mind.

"Just thought you should know," Ms. Lynne finished. She obviously had mistaken Jay's silence, his being annoyed for the opposite reason that it was intended.

Jay knew he'd probably been strange around Landon since Ms. Lynne had opened her big mouth. But he felt it was something he should talk to Landon about one-on-one, if at all, and he'd been busy with his kids and work, and the next time he'd be around Landon was going to be that damn fish fry with Landon's family and friends.

And strangely, very unwelcome, he suddenly felt itchy in his skin. Landon and Ms. Lynne's information bomb— true or not—had sucker punched Jay in the gut. An awkward something sat on the edge of his mind, a sense of being too big for his own body.

Thankfully, with his kids busy with exams and getting ready to go off to Atlanta, and work being busy with huge orders and payroll, he hadn't had five minutes to think on it.

When Friday came around, Jay had barely gotten in the front door before Bethany was knocking. "Hey, stranger," she greeted with a smile and a hug.

"Hey, Beths." It was nice to see her in person. He hadn't seen her in months. He hadn't realized how much he'd missed her until she was there in front of him.

"Where are the kids?"

"Getting their stuff ready." Jay led the way to the kitchen where he offered Bethany some coffee. She took the mug with thanks. He couldn't help appreciating how good she looked these days. She was glowing. Her hair was longer and her clothes much more chic than anything she'd owned when they were married. She looked every bit the city girl she was now.

"You look great," he said, meaning it.

"Thanks," she preened. "You do too. You seem happy."

Jay wasn't sure what to say to that. He knew he was much more settled these days, but didn't think he was doing anything different. *That's a lie and you know it.* The unbidden thoughts were rolling around. The ones he'd been trying to laugh off since Ms. Lynne had opened her big mouth. One emotional crisis at a time, please.

"Uh, thanks."

"Are you seeing someone?" she asked with a hint of friendly suspicion.

"No, not seeing anyone."

She eyed him carefully. "You sure? You haven't been able to talk for weeks. The kids commented on you being out a lot on the weekends."

"Oh, no. Just hanging out with my buddy, Landon. You remember Landon Petty?"

"Hell yeah. How's he doing? Haven't seen him since he was—what, twelve, thirteen?"

"Probably. He's good. He's working for his daddy."

"Well, it's good y'all are hanging out. Is he still a loner like he used to be?"

"Yeah, still pretty much keeps to himself." Even trying to hide his irritation at the truth behind those words, Bethany picked up something wasn't right. She knew him entirely too well to try to hide anything from her.

"Everything okay?"

"Oh. Just remembered something from work I forgot to do." He hated lying and was sure she knew he was, but he didn't want to talk about it with her. "So, any big plans for the week?"

She looked like she might keep trying to pry, but obviously decided against it. "Not really. Just doing the family stuff. Aunt Theresa and Uncle Robert are coming down from South Dakota, so it'll be a full house at mama and daddy's."

Jay smiled at the memories that brought back. Bethany's family always did holidays big. Everyone would come from their corners of the country to stay with her parents, and they did big feasts and everyone doted on the grandkids.

"You still planning to come for Thanksgiving?"

"Of course," he answered. "Wouldn't miss it."

"Good," she said. "Good." She let out a contented sigh. "It'll be good having the whole family around."

"Sure will. It's been a long time."

"It has," she agreed. She leaned back against the counter. "We've had it good."

Jay nodded and leaned on the counter opposite her and it was like time had never passed. They sipped their coffee in companionable silence, listening to the kids bicker upstairs. They occasionally smiled, enjoying the memories the scenario brought back.

At some point, Bethany leaned in with her hand on Jay's forearm, laughing at the kids' banter. It was a move she'd done a million times since they'd known each other. But something was different. Jay couldn't put his finger on it. It was like something was missing. Like someone who wasn't Bethany should be here.

Then it struck him. Landon. He wished Landon was there. He wished Landon was leaning in with his strong, capable hands touching him.

Jay's breath hitched. *Fuck.* Why was he thinking that way? He didn't mind if Landon was gay, but Jay wasn't. He'd never thought of a man like that. Ever. And here he was wanting to replace Bethany in his presence with Landon.

What the fuck?

"You okay?" Bethany was frowning at the obvious

change in Jay's mood. Jay wasn't sure what the fuck to say. He was absolutely blown away with the sudden image of kissing Landon.

Thankfully, the kids chose that moment to bound into the kitchen. "Mommy!" Millie bounced over and hugged Bethany, who studied Jay for one more uncomfortable moment before turning her attention to her daughter.

"Hey, sweetie. Ready to go to grandma and poppaw's?"

Jay watched silently as the kids hugged their mother and discussed the things they hoped to do while they were in Atlanta. Bethany and Jay shared amused glances.

"Alright, kiddos," Jay said, plopping a hand on each of their shoulders and pulling them in for hugs. His heart felt full when they reciprocated. Pain in the ass teenagers they were, but they were also his.

"You two behave for your grandparents. And have fun with your mama." He looked up at Bethany. "And if you need anything, give me a holler. I'll be around."

"Will do," she said with a smile. "Come on. Clint, help Millie with her bags." The kids hustled out and Jay followed them to the front door with goodbyes. For the first time in recent memory, Jay realized he and Bethany didn't say goodbye in any physical way.

Which strangely didn't bother him. He didn't want to be touched by someone who knew him intimately right then. The only person who ever had known him intimately. Because that touch brought with it the firing of synapses in a corner of his brain that he didn't even know had been dormant. He honestly didn't know what lay back in that place.

He grunted to himself as Bethany's SUV backed down his driveway, out onto the road, and drove away. He shut his front door, wishing the metaphorical door in his brain would so easily close.

Nothing to be done for that except getting busy. He had plenty of chores he could handle. The southern weather being what it was, the grass still grew, so he needed to mow the yard. He needed to work on that back deck he'd been trying to complete since they'd moved in.

So he got to work.

Chapter 5

He changed into his work boots and a ratty old Budweiser t-shirt. He'd only just pulled the push mower out and slid on his cowhide gloves when a familiar F-250 trundled up his gravel driveway.

His first instinct was to tense up, but the smile that stole across his face betrayed him. His subconscious was really starting to piss him off.

And scare the shit out of him.

"Yo!" Landon shouted in greeting as he hopped down from his lifted truck.

"You know those lift-kits make you look shorter, right?" Jay teased, trying to get out of his head. Which turned out to be a mistake because his mouth ran away with him. "Overcompensating for something?" *Don't joke about the man's dick size!*

Landon just laughed at that. Of course he did. His head tossed back, face beaming with amusement. "Old man's got jokes." Landon walked over to Jay and pulled off his ball cap. "How's it going?"

"It's going. Kids just left. Thought I'd do some work around the place."

"You're nicer than my old man. He saved all the chores for when I was home."

Jay let out a *hmph*. "My kids are better than most, I won't lie. But we spoiled 'em, raising them in town like we did. If I want house work done right, I'm better off doing it myself."

"Kids today," Landon joked, shaking his head in mock shame. "Who'd've thought you'd be a soft-touch dad?"

Jay scoffed. "I'm no such thing."

"Whatever you say." Landon surprised Jay by pulling a pair of old cowhide gloves out of his back pocket. "Saw you were working so I grabbed these. Mostly came over to check you were still coming tomorrow night. But if you want a hand around the place, I don't mind."

Damn Landon Petty. Damn him to hell, because right as Jay tossed all the strange shit in his mind around, as he tried to keep himself from thinking on things that confused him so much, Landon had to just… be Landon. A good man, a good friend, who no-questions-asked was willing to pitch in just because Jay was his friend and he knew Jay was doing it alone. Even after Jay had been squirrelly around him the last couple of days. And that undefinable feeling settled in Jay's gut again, making him smile but tremble a bit, because maybe… just maybe the feeling was slowly and inexplicably becoming more defined.

"I'm sure you got better things to do with your Friday afternoon."

Landon cocked his head, still with that friendly smile, and shrugged. "Not really. What better way than to help out a neighbor?"

"You live ten miles away."

"Well, you're my parents' neighbor." True enough, Landon's parents were the next house down the way about three ponds, a couple pastures, and two miles.

"In the loosest sense of the word."

"Fine. Helping out a friend." Landon's words held a weight to them that surprised Jay. He also felt a warmth he wasn't entirely comfortable with. He remembered all too well what having a crush on Bethany had felt like; the newness and the need at fifteen had been overwhelming. This feeling wasn't quite that, but he wasn't a hormonal kid. And this started in his chest, not his dick.

What. The. Hell?

He realized Landon's brows had risen and he'd begun shifting uncomfortably. He couldn't tell the man to fuck off. He didn't want Landon to leave.

He also didn't want Landon in his face right then, either. "Uh, yeah. Yes. Sure. Thanks." He motioned with his hand for Landon to follow him. "I appreciate it." He only half meant it.

He led Landon into his detached, tin-sided carport and dug out the weed-eater. "The oil-gas mix for this is in that orange can over there. If you don't mind getting around the flower beds."

"That's what you call those dirt piles?"

"Look now," Jay scolded, laughing as he handed over the weed-eater. "I had other stuff to get around to before I could do anything with the beds." Truthfully, he didn't know the first thing about annuals and what-not.

"Shame. Some gladiolas would look nice over there."

Jay smirked at Landon, who scowled. "Mama made me help her in the beds every year." The defensiveness in his tone made Jay drop that line of teasing. It also brought up stereotypes to things his fragile hold on the moment couldn't even handle.

"Well, if you don't mind doing that," he continued like they'd not made that detour in conversation. "I'll do the lawn. It usually takes me about two hours." His yard wasn't too large, dwarfed by some of the neighbors', but still took a bit of time with his finicky old push mower.

"Alright. I'll get on it." And they did. Jay's mind was blissfully quiet as he handled his task. The repetitive motions of walking in circles with the rattling mower calmed him. He'd always enjoyed working in the yard. Just being outside gave him a sense of peace, and nothing beat that smell of fresh cut grass.

At some point, while dodging an old fire ant bed, he happened to glance over, noticing Landon. Damn the man to hell. Landon had lost his shirt at some point. The plaid button down was draped over the railing on the front porch as Landon moved the weed-eater over the side of one of the large flower beds that flanked each side of the front porch.

Jay almost tripped right there. He wasn't entirely sure whether he'd tripped over the mower, the ant bed, or his traitorous tongue. Landon's smooth, powerful back flexed with his movements, sweat rolling down from his blond hair, over his neck and down toward the rise over his ass.

Jay blinked, unsure when a man's ass had become something he couldn't look away from, but there it was; two firm, round buns barely contained in Landon's threadbare 501s. When Landon moved just so, you could see his broad shoulders and rounded biceps bunch, showing off their power, their strength. And Jay could see in his mind's eye his own body wrapping around Landon's from behind, rubbing his cock against that firm ass, running his fingers over those shoulders. A trembling breath left his mouth as his body suddenly yearned to feel another person's skin against his own.

He'd never yearned like that before, and it almost made him weep with loneliness.

The lawn mower shutting off snapped his attention back to reality, his nerves roiled so hard he felt like he could vomit suddenly. Landon turned his way, his marble smooth, hairless torso gleamed with sweat in the afternoon sun. His muscled chest and smooth stomach were something you'd expect to see in a magazine, a level of physical perfection Jay had never once possessed. He wasn't anything to throw rocks at, not paunchy or anything, but he was softer around the middle, like anyone in their late thirties who didn't have time to live in a gym. His own torso was also hairy, nothing like the near baby-smoothness of Landon's.

The only imperfection was one dark brown mole just below Landon's left nipple. And nipples... Now Jay couldn't stop looking at Landon's large round nipples that were a pretty shade of pink. Perfect for sucking on.

He swallowed thickly as Landon tilted his head.

"You okay?"

No. No fucking way. I'm losing my damn mind. Jay had to swallow again to get words out, wondering why in the hell he was hard for a man, why he wanted so badly to wrap his arms around a man.

"Yeah. I'm fine," Jay croaked. "Think I need a break."

It had to just be residual effects of seeing his ex and having not gotten laid in so damn long. Right? He wasn't a teenager by any means, but men had needs, and eventually, they started making a man act a fool.

"Want me to go grab a beer?" Landon asked. Jay, grateful for a moment to get his shit together, sent Landon off to do just that.

He made his way to one of the rocking chairs on his front porch, trying to get his racing heart under control, but failed because again, he felt a strange warmth from Landon feeling at home in his house, Landon being so... domestic.

"Here you go," Landon said, passing Jay a beer. Jay took it and chugged, happy not to have to talk for a minute.

"Damn, it's hot for November," Landon complained.

You have no idea. "Sure is. At this rate, it'll still be in the 80s at Christmas." He could talk about the weather. The weather was safe.

Landon didn't respond, just sat sipping his own beer. Jay should have known that wouldn't last. "You okay? You get too hot? Need water instead?"

Lord, no. He needed another beer, not to sober up. "Naw, I'm good."

He glanced at Landon from the side of his eye, and Landon's expression held a hint of concern. Jay sipped his beer again, then sighed. "I think maybe seeing my ex for the first time in a long while messed with my head a little." No kidding.

Landon let out a sympathetic hiss. "Yeah, man, I can see that. Not that I've ever been divorced. Hell, never been with someone quite so long as y'all, either."

"Almost twenty years, altogether."

"Damn, man. I split up with someone after a year and that… that was hard, even though it was what we both wanted in the end. I can't imagine all that time, with legalities and kids involved to boot."

Maybe that *was* it. Maybe he was still just so flustered from everything. He sure as hell wasn't queer.

Couldn't be.

"It takes it out of you." They sat silently, Jay trying desperately to keep his tired brain from firing back up.

Landon put a hand on Jay's arm. Jay's head jerked to the side, and he felt his nostrils flaring. Landon immediately retracted his hand, looking sheepish. Now Jay felt like a grade-A dickhead. "Sorry. I think I'm just tired. Not much for company, you know?"

Landon nodded. "Yeah. Sorry, man. I'll get out of your hair." Landon rose from his chair and pulled his shirt on, but didn't button it up. Jay had to struggle not to lick his lips at the sight of the man's chest peeking out.

"No, I'm sorry," he managed to get out. "Thanks for your help."

"Any time. I mean it. I got most of that done. We can finish up before the fish fry tomorrow if you want."

"No, that's okay. It won't take me long. I'll get out in the early morning and handle that last bit. You got most of it done anyway."

Landon's brows were still furrowed in concern. "You sure you're okay?"

"Yeah, yeah. Just tired. I'll probably shower and turn in."

Landon studied him another minute with that easy grin of his that made Jay's fingers and toes tingle. *Please. Just go.* He'd almost beg.

"Jay, if you need anything, just call me, okay? I know we don't know each other all that well or anything, but… if you need someone to talk to." The sincerity in Landon's voice, in his eyes, made Jay only capable of grunting and nodding. He put on his best dad smile, the one he used when the kids didn't need to know he was stressed.

"Thanks again for your help," he said with feeling. He couldn't let any of the things he was feeling out, couldn't really talk to Landon about it. But that was honestly the first time someone offered to just listen to him since his mother died long ago.

Bethany had been great, but by the time he'd actually wanted to start talking to her, they had nothing to talk about anymore. Landon was just offering him a place to land. And for a man who was married for seventeen years, Jay suddenly felt bereft in the knowledge that he'd never felt like he had touched down before. His kids grounded him, gave him perspective. Bethany had been his friend and his confidant. But he'd never felt …

"What are you fucking doing?" He snapped at himself as he watched Landon's truck pull away.

This was ridiculous. He was struggling because of his ex, and the fact that he was alone today. He was off balance because he'd found out his one friend might be gay and it was just making him try to figure out how he felt about that. He was good.

He finished the last of his beer, picked up Landon's, and headed inside.

Borrowing Trouble

Chapter 6

Jay's guilty conscience got the better of him after he'd had some time to shower, eat, and veg out in front of some Andy Griffith reruns on a local station. He did what he was best at, one of the things Bethany said distanced them back when they'd tried counseling; he'd compartmentalized, as the doctor called it. He could almost hear them telling him he needed to not just rationalize and neatly put away his feelings, but what else could he do? Give himself an ulcer?

His daddy had always been an anxious man, lost in his head and unable to see past things that stressed him out. His daddy wasn't one for talking things out or sharing his feelings, getting things off his chest. Of course, that probably hadn't helped the issues that lead to his heart giving out at fifty.

Jay couldn't even let himself dwell on the thought he'd been looking at another man. It all made sense in the context of his being single, busy, and seeing his ex for the first time in months. There was no reason to even concern himself. One lesson he'd learned the hard way was that sometimes apologizing for being an ass was the best policy.

Landon was his co-worker and his friend, and had stopped by to help simply because he was being a good man. He owed Landon an apology for losing his mind there for a minute. No reason to examine why his conscience felt so strongly about it. Landon had said it, they didn't know each other all that well. But that was no excuse for bad manners. How could he teach his kids right from wrong when he wasn't man enough to own up to his own rudeness?

He picked up the cordless phone and dialed Landon's number.

"'Lo?" Landon answered.

"Hey, bud. This is Jay."

A beat of silence. "Oh, hey Jay. What's good?"

"Aw, not much." He stood and went to look out the french doors that led to his half-finished deck on the back of the house. The sun just finished giving up its final bit of light, the sky a light purple, sliding into black. The trees in the back swayed in the autumn wind, leaves falling to the ground.

"Look," Jay started. "I wanted to apologize for this afternoon. You stopped by to help." And I don't know why I'm doing this. "And I was rude."

"Oh," Landon said, the one word speaking volumes as to his confusion. "Um, Jay, I really didn't think much of it. Figured you were tired."

Jay felt embarrassed now, realizing while he may have told himself he hadn't, he obviously had overthought the situation. And that was something no one had ever accused him of before.

Jay didn't consider himself shallow, or a thoughtless man, but he didn't often think things into the ground. Things tended to be cut and dry, black and white, right and wrong. Life was not as complicated as people made it out to be. Even as a teenager, he'd never been one for angsting.

Now his ground was shaken. Heaven forbid Bethany ever find out, because she might punch him in the nose for being shaken up by life finally, a year too late.

"Jay?"

"Oh, sorry. Got distracted."

"It's cool. You've got a lot going on."

Just get off the phone. "Just wanted to say I appreciate your friendship lately. And while I'm probably being a little more sentimental than I'm comfortable with because my kids are gone, I learned too late to tell people I appreciate them and their help. So this is that."

"Oh-kay." Landon's drawing out the word made Jay *really* feel like an ass. Landon probably thought Jay was drunk dialing. He glanced back at his beer bottle collection on the coffee table and realized Landon might not be completely wrong in that assessment.

"You sure you're cool, Jay?"

"Yes. I'm good," he said with false cheer.

"I appreciate you calling, Jay." Landon was quiet and seemed to weigh his words before continuing. "I don't have a lot of friends around here. It's been nice having someone to kick back with."

"I understand. Things get lonely." *Shut your fool mouth.* That'd just fallen out.

Landon let out a sigh and his "Yeah" was spoken sadly. "I want to tell you something."

Jay's eyes closed. Damn, he didn't know if he wanted to hear. He didn't want to react wrong. "Okay. Shoot."

"Just in the interest of our continuing being friends. I'm going to tell you something, and I'd appreciate it if it doesn't get around because *no one* but my folks know here."

Jay swallowed thickly but made a noise of assent.

"Jay, I'm gay." The words hung there in the loaded silence as Jay's heart banged against his chest. Landon continued. "I hope that doesn't fuck up our friendship, or whatever, but I understand if it does. I just figured, you've been an open book. So ... I should probably tell you."

"That's fine. And it's okay." He meant it. He thought. "So, the break up you talked about earlier..."

"Yes. A man. He couldn't handle me living up here. He lives down in Brandon and he couldn't make it up here much because of work. And I couldn't quit on my daddy since he didn't have anyone else to help run the mill."

"That had to be rough."

"He mostly gave me shit because he thought I was a

closet case. I suppose I am in some ways. But, my folks know."

That made Jay's heart rate spike again. Did that mean, since he spent time with Landon, they thought he was too? Did Landon?

"Don't worry. No one will think you are just because you hang out with me." Jay looked at the phone, wondering how Landon had read his mind like that.

"That's—"

"No, Jay. Really. I understand. If it'll make problems for you or your kids, I get it. That's why I told you."

"I'm a grown-ass man, Landon. And it's twenty-fifteen. Plus, I think people know well enough I'm not gay. I don't mind hanging out with you. You've been a good friend to me since I moved back. It's not a problem for me."

Landon sighed on his end of the call, a sound of relief. "So, we're cool?" Okay, there was a slight disappointment even Jay wasn't daft enough to miss. But disappointment over what, Jay couldn't fathom.

"Long as you can accept my apology for being a jerk this afternoon." And that was about enough of that. "So. Fish fry tomorrow. You need me to bring anything?"

Landon laughed. "Sharing time is over?"

"We can braid each other's hair tomorrow, don't worry."

"Why, Jay, if you say we can swap diaries, I'll never understand how a woman could let you get away."

"My softer side is a new development." Landon's chuckle made Jay smile, and he was too glad they were teasing and his head wasn't going in three hundred directions, he couldn't even give a damn.

"Okay, Jay. I'm gonna get off'a here. And no, don't bring anything but yourself. Unless you want some specific beer."

They eventually got off the phone and Jay felt lighter. He felt fucking weird, but lighter. He decided to take his ass to bed. It'd been a long and strange day and he just wanted to crash out now.

Chapter 7

Landon startled when someone knocked on his front door. He looked at the clock, noting it was only a little past five p.m. He pulled his hands from the batter mix and rinsed them quickly in the sink, flicking the water off as he walked to see whoever was knocking for a second time.

He smiled in happy surprise to see Jay standing on his front porch holding a couple of brown paper bags from the small grocery store in their neighboring town. "Hey, you. I didn't expect you so early."

Jay grinned in greeting, his easy demeanor putting Landon at ease. He wondered if their first encounter after their unexpected phone conversation the night before would make things awkward between them. Obviously, Jay was as interested as Landon in getting on with life. Not that the conversation had been unwelcome or horrible, just uncomfortable. Landon had to admit, he was glad to know Jay could still be his friend. It was nice feeling like he had an ally in their small town.

"Sorry. I finished up the yard work and went into town. Stopped off at Greenlee's and grabbed a few odds and ends groceries to contribute, thought I'd swing on by, see if you needed any help."

Landon reached for one of the bags and led Jay into his home. "You didn't have to do this. My mama will probably bring more than what we need." Landon placed the bags on his kitchen island and Jay followed suit.

"Not a problem," Jay said. "You helped me yesterday, so it's the least I could do."

"You're welcome to a beer or soda. Anything you can find. Cold stuff's in the fridge in the garage. I'm gonna finish getting the catfish ready."

"You need me to do anything?"

Landon thought on it. "Actually," he opened the door that led to his garage and pointed out the fryer. "You know how to work one of those?"

Jay gave him an exaggeratedly pointed look. "Boy, you insult me."

Landon threw up his hand and dipped his head. "Pardon my offense, sir. I meant nothing by it. Didn't know if town living all these years had made you go soft."

"You're a smartass," Jay said with a laugh. "Where do you want me to set up?"

"Just take it out back there. Set up on the patio. Figured we'd eat outside tonight. I got some wood together for a bonfire."

Jay smiled. "You trying to reintroduce me to country life all in one night?"

"It's not an official fish fry if there isn't a bonfire, Mr. Hill."

"That it isn't," Jay replied. "You got propane?" Landon scoffed and pulled out the new propane tank and slid it into place in the fryer.

"Just wheel it out through the back door. I'll be in the kitchen."

They both went about their separate duties. Jay returned shortly and opened the fridge, pulling out a beer. "I swear I drink more around you."

"That's me. Enabler," Landon teased, plating some of the battered fish.

"Mostly it's because I don't have grown-up company that much anymore. Nice to unwind. I love my kids, but shee-it, it's nice to have a break."

"I bet. Don't worry. You'll get to unwind plenty with this crew. My friends will probably bring hard liquor. They usually even talk my mama into cutting loose and having a few."

"I'll be damned. Your mother drinks?"

Landon chuckled. "Not usually, but she makes an exception around Brittany and Mitch. They have that effect on people." He turned and looked over his shoulder at Jay. "You'll like them. They're absolutely city kids, but they're good people."

"And you can talk them into coming here?"

Landon shrugged. "Sometimes you just get tired of the same-old-club, same-old-bars, same-old-parties. It's nice to just hang out and not have to yell over people to talk."

"Probably easier on your voice, too."

"Spoken like a true dad."

"Sixteen years makes for a hard habit to break."

Landon finished battering and rinsed his hands off. When he turned to speak to Jay again, he noticed his friend had wandered into the living room and was taking stock of things on Landon's shelves.

"I didn't know you went to Millsap's." Jay turned surprised eyes on Landon after picking up Landon's framed diploma. "That's a—a smart-kid school."

Landon smirked. "You almost called me a nerd, didn't you?"

"Well…" Jay drawled, then studied the diploma.

Landon walked over to look at the diploma in Jay's hand. "Yes. It's a nerd school. Some people call in the Harvard of the South, but I definitely wouldn't go that far. It was challenging, though. So. Much. Writing." He still got cramps in his hands thinking about all the essays he'd written in his undergrad program.

"Landon Dwayne—" Landon rolled his eyes at the cocked grin Jay threw at him when he said *Duh-wayne* in a thick, southern drawl—"Petty. Bachelor of Science in History." Jay seemed suitably impressed, which made

Landon want to preen. Instead, he waved it off and grabbed the frame, placing it back on the shelf.

"It's one syllable. Dwayne."

"Uh huh." Landon flipped Jay off. "So how does a Millsap's boy end up hauling wood chips for a living?"

Landon sighed. "Well, Daddy's old business partner retired, then they lost a few drivers to the rail road. Then right when I thought I'd gotten enough employees in to leave, Donny—the man you replaced—decided he could make more money driving down to the Nissan plant in Canton. I hadn't taken a job yet, so it just seemed best to help out while I could."

Jay shook his head. "Seems like a waste." His head jerked up, face apologetic. "I don't mean—"

Landon laughed. "No, it's okay. I understand. Even my mama says all the time it's a damn expensive education to be squandering driving a big rig. Thankfully, grants covered most of my tuition or she'd be a lot more vocal about my decision to stay around here." Although, Landon himself was starting to want more. After five years longer than he'd intended to be doing the family business, he was starting to chafe.

"I'd want my son to take this education and better himself. Not that I think your folks don't want you to. Just seems like a shame." Jay's sympathy made Landon sigh.

"You know the men like my dad. Born and bred here, think it's putting on airs to move up and out. That's why he was all but willing to help me pay to build this house." Landon snorted. "I sometimes think the only reason he deals with my being gay is because he knows I'm not getting any action here."

Jay shuffled uncomfortably and Landon wished he'd kept his damn mouth shut. He didn't know why he'd said that. He grimaced. "Want another beer or something?"

"Yeah, sounds good." They went back to the kitchen.

"So what about you? Any trade school?"

When Landon passed Jay another beer, Jay plopped on one of the barstools on the opposite side of the kitchen island from Landon. "Not really. Before I really got my head wrapped around the fact I'd graduated high school, Beths came up pregnant, right before her first year of nursing school. Took less than a week before I was hitched and moving up to be in Columbus, closer to her school."

"Damn." Landon couldn't imagine. "That had to be… rough." Especially since Landon knew Bethany had lost that baby not long afterward.

"It was what it was. Figure we'd have ended up hitched either way. Didn't really know any different in those days."

"Yeah," Landon said and took a swig of his beer to quell his need to hug Jay right then. Jay sounded almost defeated, a little lost. To keep the mood from getting maudlin, Landon teased, "Back in the Victorian Era of the

'90s."

Jay humphed. "You'd be surprised." Okay, so Jay was taking a trip to introspective land.

"You good?"

Jay glanced up, then shook his head like he was shaking it off. "Yeah. Sorry, man. Been getting all introspective lately. I blame it on my therapist."

Landon resisted the urge to ask about that because Jay seemed to regret the words as much as Landon had regretted bringing up The Gay earlier.

"So what all'd you bring?" Landon asked, switching gears and going over to the grocery bags Jay'd brought with him. He rifled through the first bag as Jay's footsteps approached.

"Just some odds-and—" Jay stopped abruptly when Landon turned and nearly ran into him. Jay'd gripped Landon's biceps to stop them from crashing together and to keep Landon from toppling over. When Landon righted himself, they both froze.

Their bodies were mere inches apart. Landon hadn't realized until then that they were both almost exactly the same height, a fact made obvious by the fact their lips were on the same level as they looked one another in the eye. It'd take just a fraction of an inch to push their lips together.

And oh how Landon wanted it, his body thrummed with the need to press his lips to those slightly chapped, wide lips. He wanted to nibble on the bottom lip that was only a bit fuller than the thin upper lip. When his eyes flicked back up to Jay's, he noticed a mix of surprise, fear, and most definitely what could be desire burning in those brown depths as Jay's gaze zeroed in on Landon's own lips.

Landon's heart stuttered in his chest, eyes fell to half-lidded, and he studied Jay's face carefully as their breaths gusted over each other. For a split second, Landon thought Jay was going to move in, but a bang at the front door and a "Yoo-hoo! Landon! You home?" made them jerk apart.

Jay shook visibly as he ran his hand over his head, eyes wide as his gaze landed on the floor, then Landon, then Brittany and Mitch as they came into the kitchen. Landon's lungs ached, and he finally let out a breath he hadn't realized he'd been holding.

His friends came in a flurry of hugs and activity. He and Jay both pasted fake grins on their faces, and Landon was so fucking confused. He ached.

He wanted five more minutes. He wanted to know what just happened. Maybe it was his imagination. Maybe it was *his* fuck up. Jay edged close to the door, looking like he was about to bolt. But just then, in came Landon's folks. His mother grabbed Jay happily into a hug and recruited him into helping Landon's daddy get food and a cooler from the car.

Landon beat a hasty retreat to check on the fryer.

He may have also taken a moment to silently lose his shit.

Chapter 8

Landon only had a brief opportunity to kick himself and cuss himself for being a fool before his daddy decided to come out and supervise frying the fish. He didn't know what the hell had caused the moment, and he knew he'd probably read the situation wrong. He'd almost kissed a fucking straight man and he knew he was lucky he hadn't eaten his teeth.

"I'm gonna go grab the hush puppy mix," Landon said. His daddy grunted and popped the top on the beer can he'd carried out with him.

When Landon walked in, he almost wondered if Jay'd made his excuses to leave. Hell, that'd probably be best. He'd made fool enough of himself for one night. But his mama had roped Jay into helping with going through her Tupperware. Mitch and Brittany stood on one side of the island asking questions as they poured up drinks.

Jay caught Landon's gaze when he walked in, quickly averting his eyes. His friends didn't miss the exchange, though his mama went on chattering about how good Bethany looked when she'd seen her at Bethany's parents' earlier in the day. Landon's shoulders tensed so much they were practically at his ears.

"Hey, babe," Brittany said, bussing a kiss on his cheek. "Long time no see."

"Yeah," Landon said. He hadn't gone down to visit them in Jackson in weeks. Not since he and Jay had started hanging out more regularly over the last month. "Sorry. It's been a little busy. I'm glad y'all could come down."

Mitch patted Landon's shoulder, then bussed a kiss on his cheek as well, which Landon noticed made Jay squirm. Fuck, The Gay Elephant was really gonna suck for the rest of the evening. Landon's flinch at the kiss on his cheek made Mitch look at him drily and mouth *Problems?*

Landon gave the slightest nudge of his head to signal Mitch to drop it. He felt bad. These were his best friends. He'd known them since they all attended college together. He didn't want to ask Mitch to dial it down, even if his initial instinct was to do just that. He gnashed his teeth. Oh, well. If Jay was going to make it awkward, what could Landon do? Mitch was gay. Landon was gay. Landon's parents dealt, so Jay would have to as well. They were in Landon's house. Jay could get over it or get out. Hopefully, without a scene.

A small part of Landon was sad because he'd thought he and Jay could be cool. He knew it was his fault for almost kissing the man, but thinking on it, no way was it just Landon who'd felt... whatever that moment had been.

"Sun's almost down. I'm gonna get the fire started," Landon announced. Brittany and Mitch followed him out, talking about mutual friends and good-naturedly teasing about the long drive to the boondocks.

Bless them, neither one attempted to ask about the tension between him and Jay.

Everyone ended up outside, shortly, sitting at the patio dining table Landon set up for the get together. The laughter eased some of the dread in Landon's stomach, but he still felt a slight edge of discomfiture around everyone. He and his daddy worked on frying things while everyone else drank and chatted. Landon noticed a couple of times, though, that Jay was hanging close to Brittany. He didn't read too much into it.

Or tried not to.

"Landon, you okay?" his mama asked.

He gave her a startled look. "Ma'am?"

"You seem out of sorts."

"No, I'm fine." He would not cast a glance Jay's way. Could not. She eyed him skeptically. "Really, Mama, I'm good." He gave her his best smile and she didn't look like she was buying that any more than his first answer. He needed to get his mind off Jay Hill. Anything but.

"So, Daddy, how's it coming renewing the contract with Jensonite?"

"Oh, Lord, anything but work," his mama groaned. That didn't deter his father though, who started complaining about the new regulations the paper mill wanted to place on their drivers to renew business with them into the new year.

The conversation served as a good distraction.

Mitch eventually joined in. Mitch and Ricky Petty had an awkward but amusing kind of relationship, in which Ricky was uncomfortable around Mitch, and Mitch knew it and gave the old man hell about environmental regulations. Landon didn't know which made his daddy more uncomfortable; the fact that pretty-boy Mitch was just on the other side of flamboyantly gay, or that Mitch was a democrat.

Landon left them to it, making his way to check on the bonfire, which was going good now, before going inside to dig out the long skewers and marshmallows.

As he dug through the pantry, he heard the distant flush of his guest bathroom, before turning to find Jay walking back through the kitchen. Jay's anxiety was obvious, and Landon sighed.

Jay nodded toward the bag in Landon's hands. "Roasting marshmallows?" Landon wondered if he should accept the avoiding of the topic they probably should steer clear of with mixed company just outside the sliding glass door behind them.

But no one ever said Landon was always smart.

"Look, Jay. I'm real sorry about—"

"Leave it," Jay said with a glare. His posture did not promise good things in the event Landon pushed him.

Landon closed his burning eyes, feeling a keen pain

in his chest. "Can we just be civil? You can punch me later, okay."

"Landon," Jay said on a frustrated sigh. When Landon opened his eyes, Jay had deflated, cheeks pinked a little, embarrassed. "I'm not going to punch you. Let's just drop it for now."

Landon swallowed and nodded. That was all he could manage. The door behind them slid open and loud laughter from the patio could be heard. Landon turned with a grin and held up the marshmallows. "Dessert!" he said to his mama.

She smiled fondly. "Such a child." She spoke to Jay next. "We can never have a fire without this one wanting to roast marshmallows. It's been his favorite forever."

"At least I didn't make up roasted hot dogs this time, too."

"Thank Heavens for small favors," she said. "I'm just glad you've got skewers." Again to Jay she turned to speak. "He's made us mess up more than a share of wire hangers over the years just for a hot dog and a marshmallow."

"Worth it," Landon chirped, turning to Jay. Jay looked between Landon and his mother with something akin to amusement. The slight thaw was enough to make Landon's muscles relax.

"You boys go on out. I'll bring the plates," she told them. Landon and Jay gratefully fled the kitchen and gravitated back to where they'd been before, Landon frying with his dad, Jay sitting at the table with Landon's friends.

The rest of the night went fairly smooth. Mitch and Brittany regaled Jay with stories of Landon's misspent youth, which made Landon's parents squirm in their seats. Bastards.

The night wound down, his parents leaving not long after dinner and a couple of roasted marshmallows. Everyone got a little more tipsy while Landon worked to clean up. Mitch and Brittany were staying at Landon's that night, so he decided to let them enjoy themselves.

He was pretty surprised Jay hadn't left yet, but Jay probably needed to sober up before driving the few miles home. Country roads around there didn't have traffic often, but they were curvy and narrow, so drunk driving down them was not recommended.

"That bitch," Mitch grumbled, following Landon in the house.

"What?" Landon dropped the tray he'd been carrying into the dishwasher, then took the plated Mitch held. Mitch looked out the sliding glass door toward the bonfire.

"Damn straight girl comes all the way to the country on a Saturday night and still ends up getting laid."

Landon's heart stopped. He jerked his head up from where he'd been watching water push scraps down the disposal. "Say what now?"

Mitch held his hand out toward the doors and Landon followed Mitch's gaze. Brittany and Jay weren't touching, but they stood very close. Very. And Landon would recognize Brittany's *I'm getting lucky* posture as she listened raptly to whatever Jay said. He was playing the simple country man out there with his beer and his charming smile.

Landon wanted to vomit.

"He's not really the one night stand type," Landon said, mostly trying to convince himself. Last time Jay had the offer, he'd not exactly taken it up.

"Why shouldn't he?" Mitch asked. "She's hot. And she's got a soft spot for the wounded country boy routine he's got going on."

Landon scowled down at the sink, rinsing off the last of the silverware before placing it in the dishwasher.

"She always did have a thing for divorcees."

"Ooh," Mitch said, the sound almost a laugh. "Look at you being a nasty bitch."

Landon scowled again, then tossed over his shoulder, "No. I didn't mean it that way."

"Mmhmm," Mitch hummed.

"Were there any more dishes out there?"

"No. That's it."

Landon dropped a detergent pod into the dishwasher, closed it up and pressed the start button. "Awesome. That's done." *Be cool.* He went for a beer. Tonight was definitely not the night for hard liquor. No way, no how.

He leaned back against the counter in time for Mitch to grab his beer and take a drink from it. "So. You've got a thing for the straight boy, huh?"

"No." Landon yanked his beer back. "He's just an employee. We hang out sometimes, but I know he's straight." He actually managed to get the words out with some conviction behind them.

Mitch leaned against the counter beside him, surreptitiously glancing out toward the bonfire, a feat Landon couldn't bring himself to do. "Doesn't mean you can't have a crush on him."

God, I wish it was just a crush. Jay was the kind of guy Landon could fall for. He paused with his beer bottle to his lips. It was obviously time to switch to soda, because that unbidden thought made his blood pressure hit stroke level in less than two seconds.

Landon passed his beer to Mitch and went for a soda. "Nah, he's just from around. He grew up here. Moved back after his divorce and started working for daddy."

"So you said."

"You guys staying on in the morning or do you have to get back?"

Mitch studied Landon, but he must have implored with his expression enough to drop it that Mitch took pity on him. "I think we are heading out early. I wanted to stay until lunch, but she's got some project at work tomorrow tonight." Mitch gave Brittany the hairy-eyeball through the wall. "Which she would tell you herself if she wasn't making us both jealous whores right now."

Landon laughed, which was nice. He just... he knew Jay was straight, and he felt certain Jay wouldn't screw Brittany, but the situation still sucked really, really bad.

"Would it be rude of me to head to bed?" Landon asked.

"Fuck no. I'm turning in soon, myself. I smell like burned wood and grease and I drove two hours today." Mitch's sympathetic expression was more than Landon could take right then. He patted the hand Mitch'd placed on Landon's shoulder.

Landon shored himself up and went to the back door, sliding it open, but not focusing on the couple outside. "Just wanted to say goodnight to you guys. Had an early start so I'm headed to bed. Don't forget to put dirt on the fire and put it out, please."

"We won't," Brittany said sweetly. He was *not* going to be angry at his friend for this. She didn't know. But he could be pissed at Jay.

He didn't say any more, just shut the door and walked back through the kitchen. "Way to be the bigger woman, hon," Mitch said sincerely.

Landon smiled tiredly and shrugged. "Can't get mad at the straight people for… being straight."

Mitch made an inelegant noise in his throat. "You most certainly can. But you've got manners."

Landon huffed and went upstairs to his bed. He just needed the night to be over. So much for a fun night introducing Jay to his friends. And it all started because of a stupid almost-kiss. Fuck.

Landon blinked his groggy eyes open as sun shone into his bedroom windows. He turned his head, noticing the early hour. Not even eight in the morning. He usually slept in easily on Saturdays, so he couldn't imagine what had pulled him from his sleep.

He heard a car door slam and rolled his head back toward the window. Then the previous night crashed back down on him. He pinched the bridge of his nose and sat up in bed with an unhappy grunt. With his displeasure stacking back up in his chest and his mind reeling, he knew there was little chance he'd fall back asleep.

He got out of bed, pulling on a t-shirt and shorts before going to take care of business in the bathroom. He supposed the least he could do was make his friends breakfast before they left. Brittany's attention had been monopolized by Jay last night, so he hadn't spent much time talking to her. He could mind his manners for the time being. Not like she did anything wrong by flirting with an available guy.

She'd go back to Jackson and that'd be that, anyway, so he needed to just get over himself.

He hit the bottom step just in time for Mitch to come around the corner from the kitchen. "Morning."

"Morning, hon," Mitch said. His black hair stood up on end, face still creased from the pillows, so he obviously hadn't been up long. "Have you seen Brit? She didn't come to—"

"Morning, boys!" Brittany sang out, walking through the front door carrying her overnight bag. She was wearing her clothes from the night before, hair up in a ponytail. She looked a little flushed. Landon and Mitch shared an unhappy glance.

"Morning, Brit," Mitch said with a smile, probably overdoing the cheer. Brittany looked at both of them askance.

"You two sleep good?" Landon asked. Brittany's face split into a happy smile and Landon wished he hadn't asked. He was an idiot. She had walk of shame written all over her and he did not want to hear about how well she must have slept.

The acid in his stomach boiled with jealousy, his heart ached with despair. Fuck. He'd just known Jay would put her off like he'd done Felicia. Mitch's downcast gaze said he'd drawn the same conclusions as Landon.

"I'll make breakfast," Landon said, scurrying to the kitchen.

"Okay," Brittany said slowly to his back. "I'm gonna hit the shower."

Landon put a cork in his roiling emotions. This was not the time. He'd said it himself, he couldn't get made at her or Jay for... whatever. They were adults.

Okay, he could be pissed at Jay. Fuck him.

"Landon."

He glanced at Mitch, who approached him cautiously.

"You want one egg or two? I figured I'd do a fry-up." He pulled down a bowl to beat the eggs in.

"You okay?"

"I'm fine, Mitch," Landon said with steel in his voice. "I'm not mad at her. This is dumb anyways. I know better."

"Lan—"

"No. Really. Drop it." He turned a smile on his friend. "I missed you guys and I just wanna hang out and have a nice breakfast before y'all leave. Okay?"

Mitch hustled over and wrapped Landon in a quick, fierce hug. Landon allowed himself two seconds to relax into it, and was so fucking grateful for Mitch in that moment. Mitch then let him go, always knowing when Landon had reached his physical comfort capacity.

"Well, if she got to have fun last night, she gets to drive." Mitch pulled a bag from under the counter and held up champagne and orange juice. "We get mimosas."

"Oh my God, I don't think I can drink any more."

"You can and you will," Mitch sing-songed.

"Peer pressure!"

"Precisely."

Aside from good natured bitching about having to drive and a few questioning looks from Brittany, breakfast was their usual good time. But Landon, every once in a while, got stuck in his head, alternating in each instance between bitter jealousy and rage. He was pissed at himself, he was pissed at Jay, and he felt horrible for the brief moments of anger toward Brittany.

When they left, it was one of the rare times he was glad to see the back of his friends. He cleaned his kitchen and tried to think of things to do around the house on his Sunday off. But damn if he hadn't worked himself up a good mad-on.

He didn't expect an apology, but he'd made it to the point he wanted an acknowledgment from Jay that fucking one of his closest friends was fucked up.

But. It wasn't. Fuck. It's not like there had ever been a chance with Jay. Jay was straight.

But. Fuck him. He'd been a guest at Landon's house and spent the night avoiding him, then fucked Landon's friend. Fuck. Him.

Landon knew Jay's kids were gone until the next weekend, so he didn't put much more thought into it as he slid his feet into a pair of boots and hopped in his truck. He damn well was gonna tell Jay he was bastard. Landon had apologized for making the night awkward by almost kissing Jay, even though it seemed Jay had been just as close as Landon had. Landon felt disrespected, which was probably entirely irrational.

He tried to tell himself he was acting like a jealous teenager as he made his way down the road to Jay's house. But it didn't stop him.

Chapter 9

Jay tossed his checkbook register across the desk. Frustrated was the easiest way to describe his mood. He looked at the program on the PC Clint had attempted three times now to teach Jay how to use, but Jay still felt dumb. Hell, he did well to turn the stupid computer on half the time, so he didn't know why he thought it'd make it easier to try to keep up with his budget on the personal finance software the kids had gotten him for Christmas.

He didn't know why they'd gotten him the software at all. He didn't even remember the password to his email, and all of this on top of his stupid fucking hangover from hanging out with those stupid fucking kids the night before was doing nothing for his stupid fucking mood.

It also obviously wasn't doing much for his vocabulary.

Frustrated.

What a simple word for all the feelings going on inside him. He was thirty-six years old last time he checked, so he didn't know why he was reduced to angsting like he was sixteen. Self-examination had been one of those things that was supposed to make him a better husband, a better father. Instead, after last night's near kiss with Landon, it'd made him nothing but an angry, guilty mess.

That Landon had thought Jay would hit him over the near-encounter had distressed him. Then he'd drunk too much and flirted with that Brittany girl and lord knows that didn't help a bit. She was beautiful, with her long blonde hair, thick legs, and full curves. But when he'd looked at blond hair, he could only think of running his fingers through Landon's.

And what the hell?

He'd been married for almost twenty years, for fuck's sake. To a *woman*.

But you were only ever with that one woman, his traitorous mind reminded him. Fuck you very much.

He'd almost kissed Landon. He didn't even know if he was ashamed of it, or turned on by it. His cock tenting his sweatpants right then gave him an answer he wasn't sure he could handle.

He eyed the computer on his desk.

What the hell would it hurt? He just hadn't gotten laid in forever, a conclusion he'd come to after eyeing Landon's shirtless torso the other day. He probably just needed to rub one out.

The kids weren't home. He was all alone.

He clicked up the browser on the computer. He'd never done this, looked for porn on the internet. But even he couldn't fuck that up, right?

He did a Google search and found a free site. He felt a little bad for it, but hey, desperate times.

When he brought up a video, he watched it almost clinically. It was a strange sensation. Yeah, he was hard, and it was sex. Sex was good.

He did roll his eyes a few times, though, knowing some of what he saw was shit he'd never have been able to get off doing. That made him change the video. When the next one started to play, he watched carefully. Again, he rolled his eyes at the over the top moaning of both participants.

A strange thought crossed his mind, though.

The internet hadn't been a thing when he was a teenager, and if his folks had caught him with a skin mag, he'd have been toast. He'd seen a couple pornos, obviously, but by the time it would have been something he was into, he was getting regular sex from Bethany. Who needed porn when they had the real thing?

So he'd never... strayed. He'd never looked at anything other than standard old man-on-woman porn. He didn't know why, or what had his fingers pecking out the words *gay man porn* in the search box. But... if nothing else, it'd prove a point. He wasn't gay, therefor, gay porn would do nothing for him.

He looked through the thumbnails until his eye caught on one with a smooth, muscled blond man. He didn't let himself think on why he was looking at a porn with a guy that looked like—no one. It was a passing resemblance at best.

The video started and holy shit. The action started right away. The blond man was sucking— He clicked the window closed. His body shook, cock pounding with need. But…

Way to prove a point, asshole.

He leaned forward, elbows on the desk, and dropped his head into his hands, trying to even his heavy breathing. This was insane. His heart raced and he could feel a flush from his ears to his chest. It was all arousal. All visceral need and he didn't know how to shove this back in the fucking box. The stupid box he'd opened.

His body was so hot, sweat clinging to his brow. Granted, he'd already been hot, had taken off his shirt earlier because with it being so late in the year, he felt silly turning on the central air. Now, though, it was all because he was… well, *hot*. And bothered.

A knocking on the front door made him look up from where he'd been hiding in his hands. The knock was firm. Not angry, but definitely someone on a mission. He scrunched his brow in wonder over who'd be stopping by so early on a Sunday morning. Hell, most people he knew were getting ready to head to Sunday school at church.

He stood, only to realize he was still hard enough to pound nails, and his old sweatpants weren't doing shit to hide the problem. He grabbed his t-shirt shirt from where he'd laid it on the back of his chair and held it in front of himself. Wouldn't be the first time he'd answered the door shirtless, and at least he could hold it in front of himself to hide his hard-on.

He started thinking of anything random he could, trying to calm his body so he wouldn't embarrass himself, but when he threw open the door and saw Landon there, his cock gave a happy jump. Goddamnit.

"Uh, Landon?"

The man looked pissed. And ridiculous. In a shirt whose sleeves had been cut off, gym shorts, and muddy work boots, he looked like he'd rolled right out of bed and driven straight to Jay's.

"Can I talk to you?"

"I… Yeah, I guess." One would think with the tension between them, the anger radiating off Landon, Jay's ardor would cool. Unfortunately, his body reacted the opposite of that.

He shut the door and leaned his forehead on it, counting to ten. Landon's boots clomped on the hardwood floors as he paced.

"Look. Jay, I know I fucked up by almost kissing you. But my best friend?"

Jay jolted with surprise. "What do you mean?" He knew damn well what the man meant. He turned to Landon, still holding his shirt in front of him, desperately wishing he could put it on. He felt more vulnerable than he was comfortable with, suddenly.

The anger morphed to a raw hurt when Landon turned to face Jay, his eyes red and sad. "I get it. You are uncomfortable around me. I did a dick thing and almost kissed you. I've misread our friendship more than once. I'm sorry. But really? Anyone but my best friend. Because now I'm so mad at her for fucking you, I can't see straight."

Jay's jaw dropped. "*Fucking* me? What are you talking about?"

Landon glared. "She came waltzing in this morning with her overnight bag."

"Well, I don't know, maybe because she stayed over? When I left her, she'd passed out on the couch because she was trashed. She went in to pee and she was out when I checked on her."

Landon stilled, frowning. Jay wanted to reach for him, to run his thumbs over Landon's pinched brow. And he fucking hated that he wanted to.

Then Landon's brows shot up, eyes widened. Jay realized he'd dropped his bunched up shirt so his hard-on was plainly visible. "Uh." Jay couldn't form words. Landon's gaze flicked between Jay's mouth, his eyes, and his hard cock, which was decidedly interested in the way Landon licked his pouty lips.

A shaky breath left Jay's body, his heart thumped in his ears as a need he'd never known roared through him. He was terrified and turned on at the same time. Landon was so close Jay could reach out and touch him. That seemed to be happening a lot lately.

"Jay," Landon said, voice raw with confusion and need. The hunger in his eyes burned into Jay's skin and Jay's swallowing practically echoed in the quiet room. His mouth was so dry, his tongue felt thick. He didn't know what to say, what to do.

But he knew what he needed.

What he couldn't deny he wanted if he tried, not with the way his cock had the elastic waistband of his pants pulled away from his body, he was so hard.

Landon stepped closer to him. "You didn't..."

"No." He couldn't believe he got the word out, or why it even mattered. But suddenly Landon was there and was all he could see or feel, and the room felt small and his skin felt too tight. Even when he'd lost his virginity, his body hadn't been this excited or trembled so.

The heat from Landon's skin was easy to feel this close, and Landon's step had put him close enough that Jay's clothed cock—just the tip—pressed into Landon's crotch. A groan rumbled up Jay's chest and his whole body quaked.

Then his brain shorted.

"Landon," Jay said on a breath. He swallowed again. "Touch me. Please." He sounded fucking gutted with need, even to his own ears. Landon's pupils blew and he reached out a hand, grasping Jay's cock. Jay's head fell back against the door with a thud and he moaned. *"Jesus."*

"God, you're so hard... for me." Landon sounded

confused. He may as well join the club because Jay didn't know what was going on, but he had to have more.

"Landon, please." *God, what are you saying?*

It didn't matter, not at this point. Landon plastered himself to Jay and their lips banged together, almost painfully, as they ate at each other's mouths. Jay had never, ever felt like this. This wasn't getting off as a biological imperative, this was deep down, never-knew-it-could-be-like-this, need.

"Oh, Jay," Landon moaned into their kisses.

"I don't know what… I don't know." Jay really had no clue. What to do, how to go about this, why he was coming apart like this. But he couldn't stop it.

"I've got you," Landon promised.

Landon dropped to his knees and Jay had never seen such a glorious thing. Landon gave a quick tug and Jay's cock fell out of his sweats, long and hard, the tip red and leaking.

"Fuck," Landon groaned, kissing the head. Jay's entire body quaked. "This is beautiful, Jay." And with that, he took Jay in his mouth. His lips worked Jay over, hands fondling and stroking. Jay had never particularly cared for blowjobs, could take them or leave them. Not so when Landon did it. He thought he might die if Landon ever stopped.

"Jesus, Landon. Jesus fucking Christ."

Landon looked up through long, blond lashes, watching

Jay as Jay came undone much more quickly than he ever had. This wasn't his usual slowly coaxing out of an orgasm, the sometimes inability to even get close that had made his ex insecure sometimes. This was a tingling, blessed, pulsing hum in his body. Landon rolled Jay's balls with his hand and Jay could feel Landon's own cock fall out against his bare legs, his sweats having long ago fallen to his ankles.

Landon started grunting, shooting vibrations up Jay's cock. Jay looked down and was shocked at how delicious it was to see Landon pleasuring himself as his pink lips stretched over Jay's fat cock.

Landon suddenly grew more voracious, whimpering, and Jay gave into the urge to run his fingers through Landon's hair. It was so smooth. Landon looked up, almost adoringly at Jay, then his eyes fluttered shut as he orgasmed and shot his cum on Jay's shin.

And Jay was fucking done. His body bunched up and he practically hollered as his balls, which Landon jiggled with the tips of his fingers, pulled up. "Fuck, I'm cumming. I'm cumming."

And he did. He lost it. That door in his mind he'd been shutting off, the one he hadn't even known was closed, blew off the fucking hinges and all those synapses fired as his cock emptied into Landon's mouth. Landon hummed his pleasure as he swallowed everything Jay had to give.

Jay let go of Landon's head and Landon came up to standing, looking uncertain. All Jay could come up with as his body still sang was, "I didn't know." He said the words in wonder, in awe of what had just happened. This felt almost like a religious experience. "I didn't," Jay said. And he was scared shitless, so he pulled Landon in for a kiss to shut up his mind and keep him from asking questions. He wasn't ready for any shame to settle in or to give up at the moment.

Tasting himself on Landon's tongue was heady, and knowing Landon had swallowed his load had his cock trying to stay hard. Fuck.

When their lips parted finally, Landon lay his forehead on Jay's and Jay wanted to freak out. But a tear slid down Landon's face from his closed eyes.

"Please don't hate me," Landon whispered, keeping his eyes closed like a kid hiding from the big bad wolf.

Jay gave in to his instinct to pull Landon in. "I don't. I don't." He didn't. He was fucking terrified and confused and lost and so many fucking things. But he didn't hate Landon. But they'd have to wait until his brain was back online to sort this out. So for now, he'd just hold Landon, because it might be the only time he did it without hating himself.

Chapter 10

By unspoken agreement, after they'd righted their clothes and tucked themselves away, Landon went home. He was surprised when Jay wrapped his hand behind Landon's head, carded his fingers through the hair back there, and pulled Landon's head down to place a soft kiss on Landon's forehead.

The kiss felt like a goodbye, an apology. And Landon feared what that apology might be for. He'd driven around the dirt roads behind their houses for hours trying to make sense of what had happened.

It'd been almost scary how much he'd needed to be with Jay, how much Jay had needed in return. He'd felt every tremor, every gasp from Jay. The energy had been intense. Their goodbye had been as charged as the sex.

Landon feared he'd fucked up, royally. Now he knew how Jay tasted, how sweet he looked when he came. Landon craved the man with a fierceness that hurt.

So when Jay called out on Monday, telling Ms. Lynne he was sick, Landon prepared to mourn the friendship. He knew Jay wouldn't say anything to anyone. But he was horrified Jay might hate him, even though he'd said he didn't.

Tuesday rolled around with no word from Jay, and Landon decided it was probably best to forget their encounter ever happened. It'd been an emotionally charged moment and Jay'd not gotten laid in forever. Maybe shit just got carried away.

Either way, it made no sense and Landon felt like garbage. Of course, he figured that was what it got him for hooking up with a straight man, or at least, one who was so buried in the closet he didn't know he was gay or bi, himself.

But, it started the deep down itch to maybe get the fuck on out of Stewart, Mississippi, once and for all. He'd helped out as long as he could, and his mama and Jay were right. He was wasting his abilities and his brains, and he'd never find someone to be with if he stayed there. Hell, he didn't even have a friend's shoulder to cry on right then, unless he wanted to drive a couple hours. Since he had to work so early the next morning, there was no way to go see Mitch.

He grimaced as he looked at himself in his bathroom mirror Wednesday morning, realizing he should at least tell Mitch that Brittany hadn't hooked up with Jay. He knew Mitch probably had given her some kind of shit for it on his behalf.

After he got ready for work and armed himself with a thermos of coffee, he set out in the dark, early morning. One thing he disliked about his job, he had too much time to think, to be alone. Once upon a time, that'd been ideal. It kept him from having to be around some of the local guys that worked for his dad. Unfortunately, too much time to think right now was not doing much for Landon's psyche.

He drove down the deserted stretch of Highway 82 until he reached the turn-off for the saw mill. He parked his truck in the usual place beside the office and gathered his jacket and thermos. Before making it to his rig, though, he noticed a light on in the office. He wondered briefly if someone stayed late, but that was unlikely.

After he tossed his things in his rig, checked his log books, and made sure his trailer for the morning was loaded down and ready for the three hour haul down to Laurel, he made his way to the office to make sure it'd been locked up, at least.

He frowned when he found the door unlocked. If his dad made it in first, there'd be hell to pay. He pulled the door on open and twisted the lock on the knob, but came up short when he heard the light sounds of music coming from one of the offices. He stepped in, wondering if maybe his daddy had come into work early. He couldn't recall the last time his daddy pulled an all nighter since Landon's mama put her foot down a few months back. Now that they had Jay around to manage the mill, his daddy needn't lose sleep.

He walked back and realized quickly that his daddy wasn't in, his office was still dark. But the door to Jay's office was slightly ajar, light on and a Sheryl Crow song playing in the background. He started to make his presence known, but thought maybe he should just leave Jay to it. He smiled sadly to himself as he peeked in the cracked-open door. Jay sat at his desk, humming along to the song, writing notes in a ledger.

Landon turned to leave when Jay's voice rang out. "Come in if you're coming, Landon."

Landon couldn't gauge Jay's mood by his mild tone. A tiny piece of his silly heart hoped the way Jay's words sounded had been with a hint of amusement. He pushed on the door and walked in.

"Sorry. The light was on and the door was open. Thought I'd make sure someone hadn't been dumb enough to leave the office unlocked." Landon shuffled from foot to foot with his hands in the pocket of his jeans like a kid expecting to be scolded. "Didn't want daddy starting the day pissed off."

Jay finished scribbling in his ledger, then dropped his pen and leaned back in his chair. Jay's tired smile and guarded eyes still gave nothing away. "Never good to have Ricky starting out the day with a thorn in his paw." Jay stretched, diverting his eyes from Landon's. Landon took in the sunken cheeks and dark circles under Jay's eyes. Maybe Jay had actually been sick and not just avoiding Landon.

"Yes, I was actually sick."

Landon tried not to balk at Jay's having read his mind. "I feel kind of bad for wondering." Landon looked down, self derisively.

"Well, I wasn't *just* avoiding you," Jay smirked. At least his tone finally gave away a little humor. Landon huffed a chuckle and looked up at Jay through his lashes, not sure if he wanted to get into a heavy conversation first thing in the morning. He definitely didn't want to corner Jay if he was tired and not feeling well.

"I get these real bad headaches sometimes. They make me nauseous. Woke up two days in a row with one. I'm pretty much good for nothing but sleeping." Jay looked Landon in the eye. "I wouldn't let personal shit affect my job, Landon. That, I promise you."

"I…" He flinched, remorse settling in. He couldn't say he didn't think Jay would, because he'd obviously thought so over the last couple days. "Sorry."

Jay shrugged it off. "Look, Landon…"

Landon pulled a hand out of his pocket to hold it out in front of him. "Don't even worry about it." He didn't think he could hear the blow-off. He'd already started licking his wounds the day before, no need ripping them open again.

"No. I need to say this."

Great. Landon tried to set his face in the most impassive mask he could, then gave a single nod. Jay sighed and stood from his chair, coming around to the other side of his desk, leaning against the corner of it as he looked at Landon evenly.

"Jay, it's really no big deal."

"No big deal?" Jay's booming voice echoed off the walls. Jay shrank back, lowered his tone. "No big deal, Landon? I'd say it's… yes, it's a big deal."

"I get it."

"Do you? Because I don't." Jay's lost expression hurt to see. "I don't get how someone my age could not know something like this."

Landon's head popped up, surprised. "Know what?"

"That I like a man." Jay's hands fluttered in front of him as he searched for his words and Landon would have smiled under any other circumstance at how cute the man looked in his confusion. "Like that."

Don't get ahead of yourself. Landon's heart fluttered in his chest, nerves clenching his stomach. "Like that?"

Jay's lips thinned.

"Jay?" *Don't push.*

"No one will understand," Jay said, barely a whisper. Landon's chest ached for Jay. If Jay said the word, Landon would hug him right that second, but he didn't imagine the moment was right.

"I still have a bit before I have to haul out. Why don't you start from the beginning." When Jay opened his mouth to protest, Landon shored himself up and took only a fraction of a step closer, going for supportive presence, not overbearing. "You won't hurt my feelings." *I hope.* "And I'm the one person who won't judge you. I'm not trying to push you, but you obviously need to talk about it."

"Here, though?" Jay looked around the office.

"Neutral territory, I figure."

Jay snorted like he didn't quite think as much.

"Or tell me to fuck off. I'll understand. I just—we're friends, right?"

Landon didn't like that Jay had to think on that, he wanted to snarl at Jay's dubious expression. He almost fled, he definitely didn't need this shit. Things were uncomfortable, and just because Jay hadn't punched Landon's lights out yet, didn't mean he wouldn't if he felt cornered.

"Yes. We're friends. This is just a lot to take in and part of me wants to kick your ass." Landon winced. "Because I feel things for you, Landon. And I'm remembering things I hadn't ever really thought on."

Landon tilted his head in question and Jay rubbed his palm over his forehead. "Landon, I'm a simple guy. A redneck, if you wanna go that far."

"I don't think that, Jay."

"Either way, I'm not educated or worldly. I don't like to overanalyze things, I don't get in my head. In fact, that was a huge problem in my marriage. I don't talk things out, because I really don't have anything going on upstairs to talk about." Landon thought that was the dumbest thing Jay'd ever said, but he refused to break the spell that had Jay spilling his guts. He obviously needed it.

Jay's eyes beseeched understanding. "One time, it was even mentioned I might be on some spectrum of something-or-other, until the marriage counselor decided I just compartmentalized." Jay shook his head. "All that money and all those big words and it didn't even save my marriage. Maybe I am just queer."

"Or maybe it just didn't work out. Things don't sometimes."

Jay didn't seem convinced. "Either way. My daddy was a worrier. My mama said he'd worry himself into the ground. Then he did. Dropped dead of that heart attack, barely fifty years old." Landon remembered the old guy. He'd been a mean old cuss with a permanently scowling face. "It made him downright mean, the way he worried and carried on. I wonder if he himself hadn't seen a damn doctor and gotten on something, maybe his anxiety wouldn't have been so bad."

"That's a worldly observation." Landon didn't know why he teased, Jay didn't even respond.

"I decided long ago that I didn't want to be like him, didn't want to worry to death and over think everything, didn't want people always having to worry about me. So I don't borrow trouble." Jay looked hard at Landon. "That's why it's the damnedest thing that the last two days, even sick and puking, I couldn't quit thinking about you. The whole damn time."

"That's flattering," Landon said flatly.

Jay's scowl should not have been as cute as Landon found it, and he wanted so badly to kiss it away. And that's exactly what he should be avoiding. He couldn't be Jay's punching bag, he couldn't fall for him. Well, fall harder for him. But he could be Jay's friend. He could be Jay's sounding board. Right?

"Look," Landon started. "I think maybe you're just stressed, and maybe you're gay or bi or whatever, but it's not the end of the world, right?"

"Not the— Landon, I have kids and an ex-wife who would feel betrayed. This stuff I'm saying to you, this thinking about you, I never did this for her. I didn't think there was anything to say. I thought either I was defective or she was being dramatic." Damn. Landon spared a moment's sympathy for Bethany. And for Jay.

Jay started pacing suddenly and Landon took a step back. "Then I remember my mama. She was like a Tammy Wynette song. She always made sure I toed the line, fussed at me if I bothered my daddy. 'Don't wanna worry him, son.'" Jay made a disgusted sound. "I remembered this boy I used to hang out with all the time. We'd go fishin' and ride the roads on our bikes together. I was about fourteen or so."

Landon shrugged to show he didn't get the significance as Jay turned to him with a heavy gaze.

"Sammy Green. We did everything together one summer. He was even the first person who told me about jerking off." Jay's cheeks pinked. "My mama told me hanging out with Sammy was starting to worry my daddy, he wasn't a good influence. I didn't get it. But I was so used to listening when she said things like that, I just went with it. He moved away not long after I started dating Beth that year." Landon frowned. Jay looked at him sadly. "I didn't get why he was so sad. I didn't get it."

Ouch.

"But now I do. I get it. I get why my mama thought that. I get why it made Sammy sad." Jay's sorrowful expression hurt to see. "I get why I put that stuff away."

"Jay, what're you saying?"

Jay looked up, eyes wide and questioning. "Did I compartmentalize *that*? Did I put that away like the rest and now it's just coming back up like all these words?" Jay went rigid. "Why am I even still talking?"

"Seems to me, you've got a lot to say," Landon said softly.

"Never did before." Landon couldn't help laughing at Jay's petulance.

"Seems you took more from that counseling than you thought."

"Lotta good it's doing me."

Again, ouch. Jay flicked a guilty glance Landon's way. "I didn't mean it like that. Well, maybe, but damn, Landon."

Landon almost passed out from nerves and need and hope when Jay was suddenly there in his face, hands on both sides of Landon's neck. "I can't get you out of my head. And I can't stop wanting you. And I don't want to hurt you. And all I could think about was talking to you." Jay studied

Landon's face, eyes darting around desperately. "Sending you home the other day was the hardest thing I've ever done. And I mean ever."

Landon's tongue stuck to the roof of his mouth and his eyes welled up. God, he couldn't do this. Jay couldn't make promises, but Landon couldn't help wanting them. He'd never ached for someone like this, body and soul. He'd never wanted to help someone so much. He feared he might break from it.

"Jay," Landon whispered. Jay pressed his mouth to Landon's, and Landon's whole body sang as he was pushed back into a shelf. The wood dug into his back, but Landon didn't care as he gripped Jay's forearms and sucked on his tongue.

They kissed like that for a few moments, Landon feeling lost to the man, until Jay pulled back, wide-eyed. The wonder there gutted Landon. Could Jay really have repressed himself that long and that hard?

"Jay, I have to go soon." He hated to leave, but he was already behind schedule and he needed to clear his head, which would never happen trapped in that small room with Jay.

Jay reluctantly dropped his hands. "Yeah." His voice was rough until he cleared his throat. "I'm sorry. I'm losing it."

"No. Don't apologize."

"I don't want to use you. You just put me at ease.

It's like having Sammy or…" He flushed again. They didn't have time to get into any more random word vomit now.

"I think your head and your heart need a break," Landon said. He reached out and gave in to the need to rub the place where Jay's brows knitted together. "I'm going to give you an option. It's up to you whether or not to take it."

Another dubious look from Jay made Landon chuckle. "Okay."

"So, I'm willing to be your sounding board. I'm not going to judge you." He sighed. "I'll be honest, I think about you a lot too. But I want what you think is best for you. I know you have a lot at stake. Just know, my door is open. I'll be home tonight. Your kids are away. If you want to come to my house and just hang out or talk. I'll even kiss you again if you twist my arm. But you have to make that choice." He took the chance, in case it was his last, to run a hand down the side of Jay's face, rubbing his thumb over those thinned lips. "If you don't, I won't be angry. I won't cry in my beer. I'll understand." *I hope.* "We can be civil and pretend nothing happened. Or you can nut up and figure your shit out."

Jay's eyes widened in surprise.

And Landon left it at that. No goodbye kiss. He pulled his hand away and straightened his shirt and ball cap, then left with as much dignity as he could.

He knew he'd done the right thing, but he wanted to beg Jay to come over. Which was dumb because not twenty-four hours ago he was determined he should be done with it

100

all. But if there was a chance, even at just helping Jay figure his shit out, he'd take it.

Or maybe he'd just been lonely too long and felt that connection with Jay. Fuck.

He'd see tonight.

Chapter 11

Jay felt wrung out. Between his godawful headaches, his uncharacteristically racing mind, and his emotional conversation with Landon that morning, he probably could go back to bed and sleep for a week.

Thankfully, work kept him fairly occupied most of the day, catching up with paperwork kept him busy between sorting out equipment issues and helping Ms. Lynne sort out the last few day's stacks of mileage logs. She'd asked him more than once if he was sure he was up to being back at work, so he must have looked worse than he'd thought.

Of course, by the time he'd gotten off work and headed home for the night, he'd been awake and working for over eighteen hours.

Landon's offer to come over, even if just to talk, tempted him as he made the journey to his house. There were things left unsaid, yet he'd said more than he ever had in one sitting. He felt a keen guilt that he'd never been that open with his ex-wife. But he felt a comfort around Landon that he'd only felt a couple of times in his life.

He hadn't told Landon about the time he and Bethany almost split up between her miscarried first pregnancy and her second a couple years later. They were miserable and fighting the better part of a year after the miscarriage and Jay stayed later and later at his job, welding at a machine shop back then. He said it was to earn extra money, but in reality, he'd made another friend like Sammy.

Neil Palmertee had been big and loud and full of life. Jay thought the man was funny and his down to earth attitude was addictive. Jay couldn't stay away. Again, he hadn't gotten the implications, the strangeness that his being around another man and thinking the man's twinkling eyes were so addictive didn't exactly fit with his being 100% heterosexual.

He'd told Neil things, shared with him in ways he'd felt guilty about at times when Bethany had accused him of being distant. Again, he'd thought it was about men talking about certain things with other men that they didn't talk about with their wives. That was the way of the world, according to his folks. But thinking back on it, Neil had been his confidant, Bethany an afterthought during that time.

He'd been on the phone with his mother one time, checking in as he did, and he must have mentioned Neil one too many times because she'd been quick to start discussing his failures as a husband. She brought up, again, how he'd worry his daddy if things with Bethany didn't get back on solid ground.

Jay had been more than a little bitter toward Bethany for having spoken to his mother about their marriage. Bethany knew how easily the woman could guilt him back into toeing the line. That'd almost led to them splitting up, but he'd stayed away from Neil after that. He'd found another job shortly after, to avoid the temptation before even knowing exactly what that temptation had been.

All these years later, he felt guilty for having been so angry at Bethany. He felt even guiltier for not realizing how in the dark she'd been. But she couldn't know something he himself hadn't understood.

And now he wished he'd never clicked on that goddamned porn. He wished he didn't know what it was like to be *touched*. Because his mind was a flurry of activity, his skin a bundle of need.

After he'd gotten home, showered, and eaten, he felt slightly better. But his body wouldn't simmer enough to let him sleep any time soon. And there was an open invitation that lingered in that traitorous place in the back of his mind. That damn place had been dark, the door shut for so long, now it was wide open and had a big fluorescent bulb blinking.

He wanted.

Jay wandered upstairs and looked side to side as he stood in the hallways. The doors that opened to his kids' rooms hung open, revealing the surprisingly clean rooms. Little bits of personality lay about each room. His heart was full when he thought about his kids and how great they'd been over the divorce and Bethany being so far away for now. They wanted him to be happy, even if little Millie still occasionally mentioned wishing Jay and Bethany could reconcile.

Could he do this to them? Was it worth even

exploring whether he was as into Landon as he feared he may be?

Okay, so maybe they'd passed that point, he knew he wanted the man. But he'd said it. No one would understand. He could barely understand. He hated even thinking he was glad his parents weren't alive to see this.

But Jay's mind kept wandering back to Landon. The way the man helped him without asking for anything in return, the way Landon smiled so easily when they spoke. Landon was smart and caring. If Landon was a woman, Jay thought he'd be the perfect step-mother.

Jay felt like shit even thinking that.

God, though, the sincere and honest respect Landon showed for how desperate Jay felt over his strange new life was bewildering in that Landon didn't expect Jay to do anything other than hurt him. Jay'd seen that vulnerability in his eyes. He'd seen it in Beth's eyes enough to know what it meant.

He was bastard enough to know he hadn't really done anything to assuage that fear in Bethany over all those years, but he wanted so badly to prove to Landon and himself that he wouldn't hurt Landon.

But he would, wouldn't he? He was barely handling this whole self-awareness thing he found himself doing right now.

He went back downstairs and grabbed the keys to his truck. He needed to get out of the house, needed to breathe for a minute without the specter of his children around, or looking at his front door and remembering the way Landon's hooded eyes looked as he swallowed Jay's cock only two mornings ago.

His cock went rigid and he cursed himself for even thinking about that.

Driving around did little to ease his mind. In fact, if nothing else, it made him more antsy because he couldn't forget that his only sense of peace lately had been in Landon's company. Which was the most confusing thing of all, because Landon was also the biggest sense of turmoil in his life at the moment.

Approaching the metaphorical and physical fork in the road, the moment to put up or shut up arrived. He could go straight and head back home, crawl under his own sheets and try to sleep. Or he could take a slight left. To Landon. To uncertainty and complications, but also to five minutes of peace and a friendly ear.

He switched off his truck's ignition and sat staring at the front of Landon's cabin-style home. A light in the window flickered from the television as Jay tried to calm his breathing. He'd rarely ever acted this impulsively, even as a teenager. But he did something he'd done well his whole life, not overthink, and he just went with his gut.

Who knew his gut also wanted to be with Landon?

He sighed and got out of the truck. Before he made it to the front porch, the light flicked on and the world narrowed down to the man who walked out the front door.

Landon crossed his arms against the chilly night breeze, because of course the weather decided to change with the hour, as southern weather was oft to do.

Jay couldn't help taking in Landon's shirtless torso, his hard, pink nipples on perfectly rounded pecs. His eyes wandered down a smooth, flat belly and followed the arrow of Landon's Adonis belt to where his cock tented his thin, plaid pajama pants.

They both stood silently, looking at each other, Landon a little uncertainly. Then Jay made a conscious decision, one he didn't know if he'd be able to turn back from, but one he didn't think he'd want to take back.

He lifted his booted foot and stepped up onto the porch.

Chapter 12

Jay kept his eyes on Landon's face as Landon backed into the house. Once they'd made it inside, Jay pushed the door shut behind him, but kept his gaze firmly on Landon's.

"Hey," Landon said gently, arms still crossed over his chest.

"Hey," Jay replied.

"Want to sit down? Talk maybe?" Landon finally uncrossed his arms and held an arm out, indicating the living room.

Jay shook his head. Landon blinked, his Adam's apple bobbing as he swallowed. Jay felt his breath quicken. He had actually intended to talk, or maybe just hang out like they used to with a beer and a SportsCenter rerun. But as he stalked closer to Landon, his cock thickening in his pants, Landon's now pointing his pajama pants in Jay's direction, Jay needed more than that.

"It strikes me," Jay started, then stepped closer to Landon, crowding him against the wall next to the stairs. "That my kids are away for another five days."

Landon nodded.

"So, in that time, I'm free to be a little crazy."

"Jay, crazy is fucking a bunch of barflies, not me."

Jay reached out, trembling but sure, and brushed the back of his hand against Landon's hard cock. Landon hummed his pleasure. "Is that what you want?"

Landon blinked, shaking his head. That vulnerable look in his eyes screamed *please don't hurt me*. Jay closed his eyes and brushed their lips together just so. "Landon, I can't promise things. I can't tell you what's going on. I'm so tired of thinking, I hurt." He opened his eyes and looked back into Landon's curious ones. "I want you. I want to touch you. I want you to touch me. I want to sleep with you. I want to not be scared or confused."

"That's a tall order," Landon said warily.

"I chose you. Tonight, I choose you."

"Just tonight?"

"I don't want to use you, Landon. I don't want to hurt you, so if this, if my being scared is too much, tell me to go or tell me to get my hands off you. But if not, I want tonight. And maybe tomorrow night."

Landon was still and silent for a moment before his arm came up and his hand wrapped around Jay's neck, pulling him down to mash their lips together. Their kiss was nothing sweet, all raw desire and need.

Landon's tongue slid into Jay's mouth and Jay sucked on it, loving the sweet hint of mouthwash and the taste he remembered was all Landon. The sweet sounds that came from Landon as they wrapped their arms around each other made Jay's cock pound with every beat of his heart.

Jay grunted into the kiss as their clothed cocks pressed together. Landon slid a leg between Jay's and started rubbing them together. Jay pulled from the kiss and pressed their foreheads together, eyes closed as the friction made his brain short circuit. Every light in his head went dim except the one that focused on pleasure and feeling.

"Come to bed," Landon said roughly. Landon pushed Jay back and took his hand, threading their fingers together as he started ascending the stairs. Jay followed closely behind him, realizing this was a line, one he was going to cross tonight. He stared at their linked fingers, then glanced up to the muscles flexing in Landon's back, the way his perfect, round ass bounced with each step.

He wanted to do so many things to that body, but had not one fucking clue where to start. He really wished he'd watched that gay porn all the way through now.

Jay was out of his depth in so many ways. He obviously got the gist, he wasn't a complete idiot, but he'd never felt like this toward sex. He'd never wanted to please someone like this, even if that made him a complete dick to admit.

When Landon opened his bedroom door, Jay followed him, looking around at all the intricately carved furniture, the books neatly stacked on all surfaces. He would have teased Landon about being a nerd again, but his mouth was too dry to speak as his gaze landed on the king size bed.

The room was spotlessly neat, save for the bed whose sheets were rumpled and unmade.

Landon turned to Jay. "You sure?" His gaze was hungry, but the restraint and care he took with Jay made any reticence Jay felt melt away. He simply nodded. Landon nodded in return, let go of his hand and reached up to help Jay pull his thermal shirt over his head. Landon's awe as he rubbed his hands down Jay's front made him feel more naked than he'd ever felt in his life. Those warm, work roughened hands that were so different from anything he'd ever known, sent chills down his back.

Landon bent his head and sucked in each of Jay's nipples, giving them a gentle nibble. Fuck, he'd never had that done. He'd used that move before, but never thought his would feel the pleasure of it. Landon came closer, his natural, woodsy scent and the smell of his citrus shampoo filling Jay's senses. His balls ached, heart thumped harder as he was consumed by, and with, Landon.

Landon hummed his pleasure as he sucked and kissed on Jay's chest and collar bones, wrapping those big, strong hands around the small of Jay's back, then dipping into Jay's jeans.

And that was the biggest difference, the thing that made Landon so addictive. Jay felt worshipped. He felt Landon's touch, the way it felt like he was actually being touched for the first time, all the way from his balls to this scary place deep in his chest.

"Oh, Landon," he said on a breath as Landon kissed

his chin, then his cheek. Landon moved his hands to Jay's fly and undid it before pushing his pants and his underwear down. They both chuckled nervously as Jay tripped up a little.

"Sit on the bed," Landon directed. Jay did as he was told and Landon kneeled before him, pulling off his boots and pants, one leg at a time. Jay's cock rose proudly, hard and red-tipped. Landon ran his stubbled cheek all along Jay's inner thighs, over his balls. Jay shuddered, his balls drew up.

"Damn," Jay hissed. "That's so strange, but it's hot as hell." The pleased look in Landon's eyes was precious to Jay. He was glad, he wanted to please Landon.

Landon opened his mouth and took Jay in hand, patting the head of Jay's cock on his tongue. It was equally the most obscene and hottest thing he'd ever seen.

"Want me to suck it?" Landon asked, stroking Jay's cock, then kissing Jay's leg.

"Please," Jay begged, voice cracking. Landon smirked. Then he sucked the head in, running his tongue around the crown, still stroking with the other hand. Jay leaned back, placing his hands on the mattress behind him. "God, that's so good."

Landon gave an *mmmmm* and started sucking harder, his pretty lips stretched obscenely on Jay's thick cock, his blond head bobbing up and down. Jay's breath quickened, skin feeling too tight over his whole body.

He felt the same steady jerking of Landon's body as last time and realized Landon was pleasuring himself.

Jay reached out to stop Landon's sucking, though he was loathe to do so. "Stop, stop."

Landon pulled back, surprised. "What's wrong?"

"Nothing. I was... I was close to finishing. But I don't want it like last time. I want to touch you too." Landon looked even more surprised, which made Jay feel like a jerk.

He pulled Landon up on top of him and kissed him until Landon had to pull back to breathe.

"Landon, don't take crumbs, okay. You deserve more." Landon's eyes flicked away, but Jay didn't miss the longing he'd seen there.

Jay didn't know if he was ready to suck Landon off, but he sure wanted to touch him, so he pushed Landon's pants down and they both laughed a little as they got tangled trying to maneuver into lying on the bed.

Jay couldn't help the swelling of affection that he felt all of the sudden as Landon, with all his smooth skin, stretched out beside him. Jay ran his hands over Landon's firm body and reveled in the newness of it. Landon obviously shaved his chest and stomach, trimmed his pubes, but his legs were covered in course blond hairs from his upper thighs to his ankles.

Exploring Landon's body felt like a privilege, one Jay didn't feel he deserved. Landon's stomach clenched when Jay ran his hands over it again, tracing down to where Landon's cock lay thick and hard against his belly. Jay took Landon's balls in his hands first, fondling them. An indrawn breath made Jay look at Landon.

The man looked so vulnerable, so turned on, Jay wished he could give more promises. He settled for kissing Landon's lips, then his throat, then sucking Landon's nipples. Landon's chest rose and fell under Jay's mouth and Jay smiled against Landon's skin as he finally wrapped his hand around Landon's cock and started stroking it. Landon's back bowed and he let out the sexiest rumble Jay had ever heard.

"That okay?" Jay asked, but if there was one thing he was confident he couldn't fuck up, it was a hand job, and he couldn't help smiling cockily as Landon nodded.

The feel of another cock, one actually bigger than his own—which was no small thing—was strange. The hard and the soft, the way it jumped in his hand making his own jump in sympathy.

Landon smirked, then took Jay in hand and started stroking him in time with Jay's stroking of his. They worked like that until they ended up lying face to face, making out like teenagers, and stroking off, rubbing their cockheads together, chuckling into their kisses when they flicked their cocks in a dirty swordfight.

Finally, though, Landon tensed. "Oh, Jay," he said breathlessly. "I'm...I'm gonna cum."

"Do it," Jay whispered against Landon's lips. Their

mouths found each other again and Landon started fucking into Jay's fist, fucking his tongue in Jay's mouth until his cock spurted, shooting his cum all over Jay's cock.

The slide of Landon's fist being eased by Landon's cum was overwhelming, shocking in how much it turned Jay on. Landon doubled his efforts and kept kissing Jay, using more of his cum to stroke Jay off and the dirtiness of knowing his hand was on another man's cock—Landon's cock—and that another man's cum was the lube that eased the fisting of his cock, made the largest, most intense orgasm of his life blast through Jay's body.

His head fell back and his knees locked up around Landon's leg that rested between them. His orgasm was so strong he couldn't even make a sound, his mouth just hanging open.

When he'd finished shooting his cum all over Landon's fist, he melted into the bed and Landon leaned over him, smirking lips red and puffy from kissing. "Was it good for you?"

Jay flipped him off. Mostly because he still couldn't talk.

He threw his arm over his face and tried to catch his breath. Landon used a t-shirt to wipe his stomach off before flopping down and gripping one of Jay's thighs with his hand. They laid like that, quiet and recovering, for a while, the only sound coming from the ceiling fan clicking above their heads.

"I can't tell if it's good because it's with a man, or

because it's you," Jay said into the quiet. Landon huffed next to him. Jay turned his head to look at Landon, whose mussed hair made him look so much younger than twenty-eight.

Landon rolled his head and looked at Jay with a dirty smile. "Your first taste of the cock, probably."

Jay reached out, not letting himself overthink, as usual, and put his hand on Landon's face. Landon's smile fell away as he studied Jay.

"I think it's you," Jay said. "No one ever touched me like you."

Landon looked overwhelmed all of a sudden, and Jay sure as hell felt the same, so when Landon tried to roll away, Jay went with his gut and caught Landon's arm, pulling him to lie his head on Jay's shoulder. Landon went freely and Jay wrapped his arm around Landon's shoulders.

"Let's just sleep, okay?"

Landon's only response was to reach over and pull the blankets over them.

"Jay?"

"Yeah?"

"I'm glad you came over."

Jay was silent a moment. "Me too." And he meant it. He didn't know what to think of it all, but he definitely meant it.

Chapter 13

"Big plans for your half day, Ms. Lynne?" Landon asked as he signed off on his mileage log and put it in the bin on Ms. Lynne's desk.

She glanced up from the stack of paychecks she'd been sorting through and smiled at him. "Nothin' major, sweetie. Thought I'd go see my sister up in Starkville."

"Ah, so the usual," Landon teased. He always asked that question on their half-days, every other Friday, and she always gave the same answer. Life didn't change much around these parts. Landon glanced back in the direction of Jay's office, knowing it'd definitely changed in some drastic way over the last week, though.

Landon was almost afraid of how happy he felt. He'd figured after that night, the beautifully awesome night when Jay had made love—because there was no other way to describe what they'd done that night—with him, maybe Jay'd go M.I.A. But no, Jay had come by almost every night that week.

Yes, they'd gotten each other off each time, sometimes twice, but they'd also gone back to their comfortable friendship. Except, there was touching. Sometimes, Landon would be cooking and Jay'd come up behind him and wrap his arms around Landon's waist. They'd be watching a game and Jay would put his hand on Landon's knee. He always seemed to be feeling it out, but Landon wasn't complaining. He was shocked at how affectionate the man was.

It was almost a dream. He'd always thought, back when he was a closeted kid in a small town, how nice it'd be to have someone there whom he trusted, who wanted him. He wanted someone who got his love of his small town and the country and sat with him on quiet nights with their heads leaned together on the porch swing.

He snorted at himself for being so corny. Since it was a half day at the saw mill, he'd only had to do one haul to Laurel and Jay'd only had to go in for payroll, so Landon offered to help finish Jay's deck. The weather had started cooling down over the last couple of days, so when Jay said he wanted to finish before it got too cold to work, Landon thought it'd be a good time to test the waters, see if Jay would be okay outside of the comfort zone of Landon's house.

Landon was not ready to give Jay up yet, and he feared at this point, he was already in over his head.

"Landon?"

He turned his attention back to Ms. Lynne, who arched one of her painted on brows. "Ma'am?"

"I asked if you were doing anything special." Her frown held a level of displeasure Landon hadn't ever had turned his way, even if the old bat didn't particularly care for him. She cast an unhappy glance back toward Jay's office, then back to size up Landon.

"Oh, no ma'am. Nothing special." Nothing that was her business anyway. He did his best to keep his game face on. Jay would not look kindly on Landon's mooning outing their current... situation.

"You behave yourself, y'hear?" The words loaded with innuendo did not fall on deaf ears, nor did the calculating look in Ms. Lynne's eyes go unnoticed. He didn't figure she'd cause trouble, but she'd definitely not been fooled by Landon and he had not one clue how to control any damage other than smile at her as usual, and affect his best *aw shucks* attitude.

"I'll do my best. Figure it'll be a lazy weekend, doing some chores, helping out where I'm needed."

Ms. Lynne eyed him another moment before smacking her tongue in her mouth and going back to her work. Landon's shoulders lost a bit of their tension as he fled her front office and trekked down the hall, giving his daddy a wave.

As nonchalantly as possible, he stuck his head in Jay's office. "Headed out, boss man."

Jay put a hand over the mouthpiece of the phone he'd been speaking on and stage whispered, "Have a good one." His manner stayed professional and relaxed, but the twinkle in his eye held a promise, a fondness that did funny things to Landon's heart. He tamped down on his smile.

"Still need help finishing your deck?" Landon asked conversationally. *Nothing to see here, folks.* Jay gave him a thumbs up and a wink before going back to talking to whomever he'd been speaking with on the office phone.

Landon made his way back out of the office and to his truck, tossing a few waves of farewell and good wishes for the weekend to some of the fellas.

Getting in his truck, he took a second to breathe. Damn the situation for being what it was. He finally had a guy he liked a lot, who liked him back in his own way, who appreciated the same simple life Landon did. Jay had so many qualities Landon could ask for. But a week of screwing around and getting each other off did not a relationship make. So many things about their situation were complicated, but Jay took to things like a duck to water. His almost childlike wonder in each new exploration together, in each time Landon touched him, was enough to bring bigger men to their knees.

Landon knew Jay's kids would be an issue in just a couple more days. They hadn't discussed, at all, the possibility of continuing their encounters once life got back to a normal pace, rather than the laissez faire vacation bubble they'd found themselves in over the last week.

So many of Jay's actions, his words, made Landon hopeful. Even if that was foolish. There had to be some way to work this out.

Landon didn't expect Jay to come blasting out of the closet, hell, Jay didn't even have a word for his feelings yet—gay, bi, fluid, confused. At least Jay had dropped the "I can't be queer" shit. That ship had definitely sailed. But what did they do with that?

It wasn't like Landon marched in parades, and he wasn't exactly screaming about his homosexuality in their hometown. That'd be pretty damn stupid. But people who mattered knew. Was that something they were working towards?

Landon tried to remind himself, though, that in just a couple months, thirty-six years of Jay's life had just been stripped and bared to have been completely different for Jay than the man thought. He had to have patience. That didn't mean he wasn't nervous as hell, but so long as Jay wasn't flipping out yet, why should Landon?

Because it's so much more than just sucking his dick. Landon dropped his head to his steering wheel. He had told Mitch about the misunderstanding over Brit and Jay hooking up, but he hadn't exactly fessed up to the fact he was pretty much dropping trou every time he and Jay were in the same room together. Landon didn't imagine he'd like Mitch's saying out loud what Landon tried not to say to himself.

"It's a delicate situation. It's only been a little while. Give him time, give yourself time." Landon told himself in the rearview mirror. Maybe the pitter-patter of his heart in Jay's presence would go away or dampen as they spent more time together.

He couldn't help the inelegant snort that escaped

him. That'd be the day. Seemed now, every day they got closer. And Jay was surprising Landon by actually speaking when something freaked him out, and his silences weren't loaded ones that kept Landon guessing. The only thing causing worry was the lack of acknowledging life as they knew it would change...again...when the kids came back.

A knock on his truck window startled Landon. He smiled when he saw his daddy on the other side, and rolled down the window.

"What are you doing hanging out here? Don't you got better things to do, boy?" his daddy asked with a grin.

"I do. Got lost in thought."

His daddy cast a sidelong look toward the office before speaking seriously. "Notice you and the Hill boy are pretty tight these days."

Landon went to talk, but his daddy held up a hand to stop him. "Now, I'm not accusing you of nothing. You know I try. Just remember things could get difficult if y'all were more than just buddies."

Landon glared at his father. "Why do you feel the need to have this conversation, daddy?"

"Like I said, I'm not accusing you one way or the other, son, I'm just letting you know I see Ms. Lynne putting together ideas, asking things."

Landon grimaced and flicked his eyes back toward the office. "I thought she did look a little funny when she asked about my weekend."

"You know that old biddy don't got nothing better to do with her time. She won't rightly go running around telling everyone, but even *one* person could be a problem."

"Well, nothing to worry about," Landon told him, hoping his smile was convincing, but not looking his daddy full in the eye so's to tell either way. He hated lying out-right to his parents, so he decided to go with that vague answer. Whether it flew or not, his daddy just popped the door with his knuckles twice.

"Have a good weekend, son. Stop on by the house if you want. Your mama's always asking how you are."

He tossed a two-finger wave at his daddy, smiling as he turned the key in the ignition, starting up his truck. He set out for home, wondering if he should tell Jay about Ms. Lynne and his daddy's conversation. Seemed like real life might be catching up to them sooner rather than later. But that seemed about Landon's luck on most things.

***

Jay thought Landon seemed a bit quieter than usual when he'd arrived at his house, but after they'd started working on the deck, sawing and hammering, Landon seemed to lighten up. If there was one thing he learned from his daddy, nothing eased your soul like working with your hands, creating something useful.

"We've done more this afternoon on this thing than I've managed in the six months I've been in this house," Jay said.

"Well, you know us young guys, we got more stamina. Get things done quicker." Landon winked at Jay.

"I don't hear all that many complaints about my age from you in other places," Jay snickered. He didn't know where his ability to be so light hearted about his sexual relationship with Landon came from, but he rarely found himself second guessing teasing about it. Nah, he wasn't all that overly friendly with Landon outside either of their four walls, but when it was just the two of them, he found himself more relaxed than he ever remembered being.

So many changes were happening, so much newness had been a part of his life lately, he didn't really even have time to balk at it, otherwise he'd just be sitting in a corner catatonic, way he figured it.

"So…" Jay said, turning back to measuring and marking on a two-by-four. "I talked to my old couple's counselor."

Landon's head popped up and his mouth wobbled up and down like a goldfish before he regained his composure. Jay felt a tug in him to kiss the surprised look off Landon's face, but he really wanted to get the words out.

"I don't know who it shocked more, me or the doc. Didn't do all that much talking when we used her first time around, so when I called in, she thought I may have finally snapped."

"Did you?" Landon sounded so serious, Jay felt the guffaw start in his chest before it belted out of him. "Well, it's a legitimate question."

"I thought so. I guess I was worried I was taking all this too well."

Landon's expression gave away nothing, which was a first in a while. Landon usually was particularly easy to read, especially for Jay. Jay'd decided once they started exploring whatever it was that transpired between them, the least he could do was be open with Landon. He didn't want anyone getting hurt, and it was Jay's life that was the more complicated of the two right now.

"What'd she say?" Landon asked.

"Well, I was almost expecting a referral to a friend who might be able to talk me out of my new-found attraction for men." Landon snorted. "But, one good thing about the doc being a baby—one of the reasons I'd discounted her help to begin with—she was a bit more enlightened than that."

"And?"

"She said she was worried I was compartmentalizing again." At Landon's concerned side glance, Jay continued. "She was as surprised as me when she said I was right and I'd probably just shut that stuff down so I didn't worry my folks." Jay walked over to Landon and brushed their fingers together as he passed him some of the marked lumber for Landon to saw.

"She called it Martyr Syndrome, but the way she laughed at that, I'm pretty sure she made that up."

"Yeah, but it's a pretty apt description."

"That it is." Jay stilled Landon, looking him in the eye. "I messed up my marriage by not knowing me, and by not talking. I don't want to do the same with you, only … I'm still real confused. I know I feel good with you. And I love spending time with you. So I'm trying to keep from thinking it into the ground. But she said that may be a problem, because I'm not looking at the reality of when my kids come home."

Landon sighed, sadness dripping from his every pore. "I thought about that. I've been concerned. I guess I don't want to set myself up to think this is more than it is."

Jay rubbed his hand over his sweaty brow. "Thing is, like I told you to start with, I feel *so* much when I'm with you, I want to make promises. Especially when you get here looking all sad after we had the night we did last night and get to spend this afternoon just the two of us. It feels so *right*, it's hard to let myself dwell on those who will think it's wrong."

"And there are plenty who will." Jay smiled, loving Landon's lack of ever sugar coating things.

"I'm not much further along yet, Landon. I won't lie. I'm doing my best here, but it's when I'm with you that I'm at my best." The way Landon lit up at that made Jay feel so good inside it hurt. "But when you're not here, I'm out in the woods without a compass and it's cloudy." Jay shook his head. "I have to thank you, mostly, because I know this isn't easy, but I appreciate how you aren't pressuring me. It's keeping me from retreating back in that place, just yet." Jay stopped. He really couldn't beat this conversation in the ground anymore, so he hoped Landon took those words as sincerely as he'd meant them.

Jay definitely had some guilt he was working through, on top of everything, because he couldn't remember a moment, even a small one, where he'd pushed to give Bethany half the peace of mind he offered to Landon.

"Oh, Jay. I do understand. I won't say it's any easier on me, but I guess I'm not done here yet."

Jay leaned forward, briefly kissing Landon chastely on the lips before going back to his side of the deck. He still felt the ghost of Landon's warmth on his lips as he smiled to himself. "Way I see it," Jay said, "we do this just like if I was seeing a woman." He didn't even respond to the rude noise Landon made. "I wouldn't introduce her as someone I'm dating until I knew we were very serious, especially since Millie is still adjusting to the split. I'm not that kind of man." He turned to Landon. "And I definitely might want to know how to explain the whole *man* thing to myself before I can wrap my head around telling my kids. Or my ex."

He groaned inwardly at the thought of all of that.

Enough of that conversation. All of it.

He thought of something he'd been meaning to ask. He figured it beared considering since it was a factor in all of ... this, whatever this was. "Landon, what do you want to do in life?"

Landon was silent long enough, Jay turned to check on him. Landon's brows were scrunched in confusion. "What do you mean?"

"I mean, do you want to keep working for Petty Mill, or do you want to use your big boy education?"

Landon smiled serenely after a moment. "I want to teach. Always have wanted to."

Jay blinked, tilted his head. Then he returned Landon's smile. "I think you'd be a mighty fine teacher. You're so patient. Easy to talk to."

Landon's cheeks tinted, a flush of pride, not embarrassment. "Thanks. That… from you, it's nice to hear." Jay felt his own cheeks flush at that. Yeah, it was likewise nice to be held in someone's high regard when he had so much respect and… adoration for them. He could admit it. He'd come to adore Landon in a way he couldn't yet understand or put into words. But by god, he hoped he could figure it out sooner rather than later, because he felt like happiness was just dancing at his fingertips.

Chapter 14

At some point that night, after coming in from working on the deck, their watching tv on the couch had gone from them sitting on opposite ends and eating sandwiches, to leaning against one another and drinking a beer. It hadn't taken long for even that leaning shoulder-to-shoulder to evolve into making out.

Landon hadn't necessarily expected to get laid that night. Sometimes after big conversations like that, Jay was more about just the act of touching, rather than getting off. Landon could understand it. For all that this sucked for Landon's wary heart, trying not to get attached, Jay had a whole life change to adjust to.

But Landon would admit, while he was a patient man, his dick was no such thing. So when Jay'd pulled Landon between his legs and gripped his ass, Landon had breathed a sigh of relief. They'd started with a slow grinding of their clothed cocks, then when Jay'd made sure the blinds were drawn, they were naked in short order and touching every inch of skin they could get their hands on.

Jay's enthusiasm was fun. While some things he did with the sexual knowledge of any man who'd had sex with anyone; some of the new things, he fumbled with. But his enthusiasm and near teenaged excitement for each new experience was heady.

The way he fucking worshipped Landon's body, made love to it like it might disappear on him, always left Landon not only sated, but feeling cherished. That was just as new to Landon as any of this was for Jay.

"Landon?" Jay asked into their kisses. Landon kept steadily stroking their cocks together where he'd trapped them in his lubed hands. That'd been the one thing he'd been daring enough to employ, lube. He figured it'd at least make the frotting more interesting. And perhaps it'd ease the way into eventually, maybe one day, talking about going further.

"Yeah?"

Jay rolled them over until Landon was on top, straddling him. The position was awesome because he could look down at Jay, take in his powerful shoulders and his lightly furred chest and tummy. He loved how Jay didn't have the stomach of a teenage muscle head. He had an honest, working man's build, complete with a slightly doughy stomach. But he was all power and built to go for hours, strong and sure.

"I want to try fucking. At least once," Jay stated.

Landon stilled his hands, though Jay continued fucking up into his joined fists.

"Jay, we don't have to, you know. It's not like a gay test."

Jay stopped moving and gripped Landon's waist

firmly. "I'm not worried about that. I want to fuck you, Landon. So bad. You have no idea. It's like it's just... not fucking enough, touching you like this." Jay leaned up on his elbows and kissed Landon frantically. "This is great, this is perfect. But, if you like it, I really want to fuck you."

Jay winced. "Unless you're really not into it. Then I understand."

Landon shook his head, slowly. Wasn't this a day full of surprises? Hell, Jay was full of surprises. From that quiet, simple man he'd first seen in his parents' kitchen to this almost daring, open Jay he had underneath him now, Landon was a little light headed from his wanting.

"I'd love to, I guess I just didn't think you'd want..."

"Landon," Jay said, then kissed him sweetly. "I want everything I can have with you while I can."

Landon could have done without the last few words Jay'd added to that thought, but for now, he wanted this. He wanted Jay and Jay wanted him, and Landon couldn't believe it because he'd really thought this moment was too much to hope for.

"Fuck. Jay, I didn't exactly bring condoms with me. I hoped we'd eventually discuss doing this, but... I didn't figure we would."

Jay reached up and grabbed Landon's face. "Are you clean?"

"What? Of course I am," Landon said, a little offended. Then he got it, eyes going wide. "Jay, that's… kinda big."

Jay flexed, making his cock jump where Landon still held it. "Thanks for noticing."

Landon laughed out loud. "Not that, you jackhole. I meant… going bare."

"Landon, it's us, just us. I know this is a little from being drunk on you, but I want all of you, if it's safe. I *know* I am. I haven't… with anyone… and my last stuff was all…" Jay seemed embarrassed to admit that. Landon realized that meant he would only be the second person Jay'd had sex with *ever*. Holy shit.

"Jay, I haven't been with anyone in… well, it's been a long time. I'm clean. But," he looked at Jay carefully. "You're sure?"

"We can just keep on with our hands if you want," Jay said. "I don't want to—"

"No, I guess I'm just surprised, is all."

Jay smirked. "I like keeping you on your toes."

Landon dropped down and devoured Jay's smiling mouth, pinching his nipples. They rubbed against each other like that for a while until Landon reached between them and pushed Jay's cock behind him, fitting it in the crack of his ass. He chuckled into the kiss when Jay groaned as Landon started rubbing his ass, his hole up and down Jay's cock.

Shivers raced up and down his body with each pass of Jay's fat cockhead over his entrance and Landon's body *craved* having Jay inside him. This would, in fact, be his first time to ever go bare with a man. He'd only done anal a handful of times, always with guys he'd dated however briefly, but they'd never made it to the stage where he trusted them to go bare. This, this was a big fucking deal. But he did trust Jay. Even if it'd break his heart in the end, he wanted the same thing Jay did; he wanted all of Jay, and to give Jay all of him. Even if just for tonight.

Landon leaned up and instructed Jay to hold out his hand. Jay did as he was told and Landon puddled lube in his palm. "Now, cover your cock in it." Jay's eyes were glassy from the pleasure as he worked his own cock with the lube.

"Gimme your hand again, Jay." Jay complied, and Landon poured more in his palm. "Now do the same thing, only make sure your fingers are good and slick, too." Jay looked at him questioningly. "You're gonna lube me up. Get me ready."

Jay started trembling much like he did the first time Landon had blown him. He couldn't believe it was only a week ago. He felt like he could tell you so much about the man, and he could certainly tell you every point on Jay's body to get him off the fastest. Seemed impossible they'd covered that much sexual ground in so short a time. But honestly, the emotional side, that'd begun the first night they sat down and had a few beers at Woody's.

Jay started circling Landon's hole with his fingers, timidly pressing his shaking fingers against the ring. "God, so tight, Landon."

"Wait'll it's your dick, babe." He pushed back against Jay's fingers. He loved the flare in Jay's eyes when he'd called Jay babe. Landon wasn't much for pet names, but hey, if it did it for Jay, he'd call the man *snookums*. "Gimme your fingers. Please." Jay did.

Landon dropped his head to Jay's chest when the first thick, calloused finger's burning entrance was complete. "You're so hot inside, so tight," Jay said reverently. Jay started fucking his finger in slowly, then added a second. Jay wasn't a complete novice with this then, Landon figured, but he did not want to get into thinking about Jay and his ex's sex habits right at that moment. Or ever.

Leaning up, palms on Jay's chest, Landon pushed down onto the two fingers invading him and Jay gave them a twist, his smile turning devious as he watched Landon's face. Lord knows how it looked at that point.

"Fuck, that's enough. I need you, now," Landon moaned breathily.

"Thank fuck for that."

"Your mouth has gotten filthy, Mr. Hill." Landon met Jay for a tongues-out, mouth licking kiss.

"You're a bad influence, young Petty-wan."

Landon groaned and burst into laughter. "Oh my god, that was so lame!" They both laughed, but the laugh turned into a moan as Jay took himself in hand, patted

Landon's hole once, twice with the head, then pushed in. Landon sat back, head lolling as he moaned loudly, sinking down on Jay, inch by painfully pleasurable inch.

They sat, breathing loudly, eyes closed and lost in their personal pleasure for a moment. When Landon opened his eyes, he reached to run a thumb over Jay's bottom lip that he'd sucked in. Jay took Landon's thumb in his mouth and bit down lightly. Landon let out another moan, then moved his feet to either side of Jay's waist. That was all he needed to get the right leverage, hands on Jay's stomach, to pull himself up to having just the head of Jay's cock in him, then dropping back down.

"God, fuck, Landon, so fucking tight." Landon didn't even have it in him to make fun of Jay for saying "tight" again.

Landon started riding Jay, loving the way Jay's eyes roamed over his body, then down to where they were joined. Landon slid his hands under him to feel where Jay's cock was moving in and out of him.

Jay sat up abruptly and sucked Landon's bottom lip in, wrapping his big arm around the small of Landon's back and started thrusting his hips up. Landon gripped Jay's shoulder with one hand and his own cock with the other, holding on for the brutal fucking Jay was giving him. God, knowing Jay was bare in him was such a turn on, he didn't know if he'd last. This really was just them, together.

When Landon looked in Jay's eyes, he saw not only desire there, but a look full of that almost innocent fascination. He could wholly relate. There was something so intense about the moment, the way Jay trembled, the way their bodies touched in so many ways. This wasn't just fucking, but had it ever been with them?

"Oh, mother—" Landon's head fell back on a yelp of intense pleasure. "Oh, fuck right there, Jay."

Jay seemed surprised. "There's…"

"Prostate," Landon sang, silly-like. Jay laughed and kept angling his dick up. He didn't peg it every time, but Landon's prostate got enough prods to make his whole fucking body feel like his nerves were shorting out.

"Shit, I'm gonna cum, Jay."

"Yes, cum for me," Jay begged, burying his head in Landon's neck, thrusting up. Landon started helping, fucking himself down on Jay's cock, and they both made pitiful, gasping whimpers as they both got close.

"Oh, fuck me," Jay cried out. "I'm gonna cum. Right now."

Landon clamped as hard as he could to help milk Jay's cock and stroked himself harder. And within a few strokes, Jay let out a cry, his cock making those tell-tale jerks inside Landon. "Oh, I'm cumming. I'm cumming inside you," Jay sigh-grunted into Landon's neck before biting down lightly.

The feel of Jay's biting, his release, knowing Jay was filling him, marking him inside, Landon's cock erupted, shooting between them as his riding of Jay's cock became clumsy and eventually stilled.

"Oh, fuck, Jay." He fell backward, Jay's cock sliding out of him.

He lay breathing heavily for a moment before looking up to check on Jay. He half expected Jay to be a little freaked out. But the pleased, almost predatory look on Jay's face as he stared at Landon's ass was disconcerting.

"You okay?"

Jay shook his head in disbelief and came up Landon, kissing his pelvis, then just above his belly button, and up his chest. Eventually, he made it to lying bodily on top of Landon, kissing his mouth with everything he had, leaving Landon breathless.

"I take it you enjoyed yourself?"

"Are you kidding?" Jay asked with the enthusiasm of a teenager. "That was the hottest thing ever." Landon couldn't help snickering. Which turned into a moan when Jay reached and ran a hand over his sensitive hole. "Especially seeing my cum there." Jay dipped his finger in and Landon's head pushed back into the couch cushion.

"Figured you'd think that was gross."

"Hell, me too." Jay shrugged. "Usually do, only… slightly different orifice."

Landon shoved Jay, making gagging sounds. "Oh, god, please don't make me think about vaginas right now!"

Jay huffed a laugh and returned to kissing Landon.

***

Jay's cock was still a semi as they crawled into his bed that night. He didn't know what had come over him. He became such a fiend around Landon, and things he hadn't imagined turning him on before got his skin hot and tight. He had never been the type to just hang around after sex, reveling in the naughtiness of it, enjoying the staking of his claim on another person's body. And damn, didn't that thought bring him up short.

The water shutting off in the bathroom reminded him there was another person who'd sleep in his bed and that was comforting, for once. Yes, early on in his marriage, he'd loved having another person to touch base with, knowing someone who cared for him, that he cared for, was a constant. But that'd dissipated, certainly in the last four or so years of their marriage. It was officially the first time Landon would stay over with him. Aside from their first hand jobs, Landon had typically gone home later at night, but this time, Jay'd wanted him to stay.

Jay still felt a sense of awe at just how different it'd been being with Landon. There wasn't hours of work just to cum, there was a connection he didn't even know could exist. He hadn't gotten what sex could be, other than a pleasant way to spend a bit of time.

Tonight, physically, emotionally, he was sated.

Even knowing Landon had been filled with Jay had come with its own kinky, but bone-deep satisfaction that was wholly novel to Jay. It was like that back room in his brain, the fluorescent lights weren't just flickering anymore; whole sections were starting to become completely lit. And Jay's heart ached with it in good ways and bad.

"You okay?" Landon asked, as he came from the bathroom and slid under the covers. He looked at Jay carefully until Jay reached for him and pulled him over, mimicking the first time they'd slept together, Landon's head on Jay's shoulder.

Jay felt content and sated. For tonight, all he needed was his bed and Landon close by. The rest could wait 'til morning. A new day, new things to figure out. But Jay wanted to get it right, whatever it was he was doing right now. Even if he didn't end up with Landon, he wanted to know he'd done the right thing in the end. He was too old to play games, and for both their sakes, he had to really get his head together.

He'd probably be wise to go see his counselor in person soon, because he knew Landon didn't need this being dumped on him since it involved him too.

"Jay?"

Jay quieted his mind, then looked fondly at Landon. "Thanks for tonight." He kissed Landon on the forehead. Such a simple thing, but it made Landon look at him like he hung the moon. Yeah, that's definitely all he needed tonight.

"Night, Landon."

And easily, they slept.

Chapter 15

The day, Landon must admit, had been perfect. They'd started early, he and Jay, waking in the same bed, warm and content. After quick handjobs, showers, and a simple breakfast, they'd set to work, finishing up Jay's deck. The day had been more brisk than the previous, so shirts and hooded sweatshirts stayed on, but that didn't stop them from subtly finding ways to touch one another.

Jay's surprising affection grew more frequent, as well as his easy, relaxed smile. There was a comfort in their little place, hidden from prying eyes, out in the country. Aside from acting like horny teenagers, they had a light lunch of sandwiches, made small talk, and managed to finish all but the final staining of the wood.

The more time Landon spent with Jay, the more a blossom of hope grew in his chest. He knew the real test would come when reality and Jay's children returned to call, but sitting on the finished deck as the sun disappeared behind the tree-line, sipping coffee, made it hard to stress.

Okay, so the seed of doubt existed on the same plot as that blossoming hope. But each day in Jay's sunlight over the last week, each hour, had made the hope bigger than the ugly doubt. There were still no promises between them, but Landon had to think they'd moved to something... more.

Something bigger and more important had transpired, especially the night before. And their easy camaraderie throughout the day had to be a sign this was no longer just Jay experimenting. Even Jay's words led Landon to believe so. It was too soon to be thinking of love and Jay coming out. Hell, Landon didn't even know Jay's kids well enough to think *Oh, let me sign up to be you stepdaddy.*

Even the thought of those words made Landon shudder.

"Somebody walk over your grave?" Jay asked. Landon turned to look at Jay's smiling face, sitting like a man without a care in the world in his cheap plastic chair on his new deck next to Landon. Landon chuckled and stretched out his legs in front of him, working out some of the soreness from working so long that day.

"Just got in my head a bit. 'Borrowing trouble', as you say."

Jay huffed. "I've done enough of that lately without you doing the same." Jay fell silent and they both looked back out toward where the sun made its final descent, dipping their part of the world into night. The sound of Jay's coffee cup plopping on the cable spool they were using as a side table drew Landon's attention back to his friend— lover? Jay's face morphed into a frisky smile as he stood and came to straddle Landon's lap.

"Hello," Landon drawled. "Did you want something?"

"Thought I'd show you one of my favorite new

tricks for getting out of my head."

Landon tilted his head, wondering briefly if that meant before, Jay was too in his head during sex, but he had no desire to think on Jay's sex life with women. Also, the thought was a silly one to base any further hope on. And the warm, lightly chapped lips on the column of his throat made him concentrate solely on that point of pleasure and his steadily rising cock.

But suddenly, Jay hopped off Landon's lap with a hissed, "*Damn it.*"

Landon blinked for a moment, trying to catch up with Jay's reason for switching gears so quickly. Still a bit lust drunk, Landon just barely noticed the sounds from behind him inside Jay's house, until a light flicking on from inside startled him.

The squeaking of the French door to the deck opening, had him schooling his face much better than Jay, who looked a bit like the proverbial deer caught in the headlights. Thankfully, other than that, Jay didn't look like anything had been going on. Landon turned nonchalantly to the teenage boy in the doorway.

"Hey, dad," Clint said. Landon quirked a brow. The boy looked suspicious. Surely they hadn't seen anything. It'd been dark outside. Landon kept his face neutral, hoping Jay'd gotten his shit together unless he wanted an awkward conversation with the bouncing preteen girl who followed Clint out and flung a hug around her dad's waist. They were both shortly followed by the deck light getting flicked on and Bethany popping her head out.

"Oh, my goodness! Landon Petty? When did you get so big?" She came out, smiling broadly, hugging Landon with the same enthusiasm her daughter had hugged her ex-husband. Landon winced, but hugged her back. Clint still eyed the scene carefully, but came to hug his dad and give him a *hello*.

"Hey, Bethany," Landon greeted.

"You all are back early," Jay stated, a little dumbly, but he seemed to have recovered, curiosity being the most prominent emotion displayed on his face.

Bethany stepped back from Landon and put a hand on Jay's forearm. Landon had to bite down on his tongue as jealousy flared up in him. What could he even say? Of course she would be comfortable touching Jay. She didn't know she was being forward in front of his ... hell, Landon wasn't really anyone, officially.

"I'm so sorry, Jay. We tried to call a couple of times today when we were on the road. Clint forgot he had a project to do and everything for that class was here at your house, so I had to bring them early."

"Oh, it's no problem. We were working on the deck, so I didn't pay much attention to the phone." Jay's last statement was a little chagrinned.

Bethany looked around the new deck. "It looks great. Y'all did real good." She smiled fondly at them both, then to Landon she said "That was nice of you. I'm sure you had better things to do than hang out with this old bore."

Landon wanted to snap, deny her words. But coming off defensive was probably dumb, and Jay's eyes communicated a plea to play nice. "It was no trouble at all. We just finished up, actually." And now real life had come to call. Early at that. As Jay said earlier, damn it.

"It was nice to see y'all. I'm sure you got catching up to do. I'll get out of your hair," Landon said as he made an excuse to leave. He turned to Jay with a sad, but hopefully understanding, smile. "We got everything put away, right?"

Jay smiled back, apologetically. Thankfully, Bethany was rounding up the kids to go inside to find something for dinner, so they didn't see the silent communication going on between the men.

"Yeah, we got it all put away. Anything we didn't isn't important enough to worry about tonight."

Landon gave a nod and went for the door, but Jay grabbed his arm. He watched over Landon's shoulder, probably checking for prying eyes, before he turned his imploring gaze on Landon. "I'm so sorry."

"No. I get it. It was a while-the-kids-are-away thing." Landon didn't know why he was letting Jay off the hook for everything. Jay seemed confused by his blanket statement as well.

"I told you, even if I was with a woman, I'd take my time before telling my kids. This is a bit more complicated."

Before Landon could speak, Jay squeezed Landon's forearm. "I'm sorry our night got cut short. I *do* want to see you again."

"We'll see each other at work, of course."

Jay's brows flattened, lips thinned, unimpressed. "I want to *see* you. And I don't have time to do this any better. I just … Landon, I'm not done here unless you're saying this was all you wanted."

Landon felt breathless, chest constricting with that hope he'd felt all day. "Oh."

Jay shook his head, giving Landon's arm one more squeeze. "I'll call you, okay?"

"Is that what you say to all the guys?"

"No," Jay said seriously. Landon tried on his understanding grin again.

"I'll hold you to it, then." *Please.* He felt ridiculous, but he knew he couldn't let their abruptly shortened night be the last time he ever touched Jay.

They parted and made their way into the house. Clint had gone upstairs while Bethany acted like she was right at home, shuffling through cabinets in Jay's kitchen. To his credit, Jay didn't look any more impressed by that than Landon. Landon knew Jay was right, though. His coming out, even if he didn't label it any more than just "I'm dating a man," would be a process. Assuming Jay ever did utter those words, tonight would not be the time.

Millie perked up from where she'd posted up on one of the stools on the breakfast bar. "Do you have to leave, Mr. Landon? Mother is making chicken pot pie. Hers is the best."

Bethany looked at her daughter and shrugged at her use of the word *mother* before saying, "I'm sure Mr. Landon has better things to do than spend family night with us."

"Yes, and I'm sure your mama needs to get on the road sooner rather than later," Jay said pointedly. Bethany looked as surprised as Landon felt at the words. They weren't mean, just stating the fact this was not her home.

"I'll see you next time, Millie," Landon said, then made his goodbyes again before slipping out to his truck, doing his damnedest to keep the image of *family night* out of his head, ASAP. He decided the best course of action now would be to trust Jay, and respect Jay's need to get his own head in order. Either way, he would try to protect his heart, because whether Jay was communicating better or not, the man could realize he didn't want the drama of being in a same-sex relationship yet. Landon could just keep hoping Jay'd stay true to his word and keep him in the loop.

***

Jay enjoyed dinner with the kids and Bethany. There'd been more laughter than he remembered there ever being. Not that they were particularly unhappy, family wise. The tension between he and Beth had just made things a little more melancholy in the years leading up to the divorce, and with the kids having a little trouble adjusting to everything over the last year, had made things a bit tense for a while. Now, though, despite his feeling like he was in new skin with a different brain, he felt more alive than he had in a long, long time.

Clint's silence was a little unusual, but there didn't seem to be anything angry simmering under the boy's surface. He seemed more thoughtful; he was like his mama that way. Millie happily told about time spent doing some shopping with her mama in Atlanta's malls. He wondered when she'd started becoming such a young lady, because most definitely less than a year ago, she'd have balked at the mention of shopping even at Walmart.

After dinner and baths, Jay and Bethany took turns saying goodnight to the kids. Jay felt a twinge of guilt knowing some of Millie's ebullience came from her parents being under the same roof. He wondered briefly how she'd feel if she knew who he'd been carrying on with lately. She was as polite to Landon as she would be to any other adult, seeing as she didn't know him all that well. He didn't suspect she'd be all that enthusiastic over him dating anyone, honestly.

They'd raised their kids better than to be hateful. Even if being gay wasn't an open reality with anyone in their lives up 'til now, he had never heard his kids be hateful toward anyone because of it.

He wondered why he'd never thought to have a talk with them about such things before, but then he realized he hadn't exactly had the conversation with himself until he met

Landon and his own past had started coming to call.

After kissing Millie on the forehead and getting fussed at because a twelve year old should be able to stay up later than nine p.m., he went to Clint's room. Bethany passed him in the hall. "Hey, I'll go finish putting the dishes in the dishwasher."

Jay knew it was too late for Bethany to drive back to Atlanta, possibly too late for her to go over to her parents' house at this hour. He didn't want to kick her out, but he also didn't want her—or even Landon, really—around tonight. He wanted things back to the new normal of just him and the kids for a couple of nights so he could think. And wasn't that amusing, since he'd done his best not to do so for so very long.

He knocked and popped his head in Clint's room. "Hey, bud. You all set?"

Clint looked up and gave a good natured grin. "Yeah, Dad." He set aside his laptop and stretched. "Just working on this project. Sorry if we busted up your weekend plans."

Jay tilted his head, heart beating a little faster, nervously. "Nothing big. We were just finishing up some odd jobs around the house." Clint's face was expressionless, but he shrugged. "Did you have fun in Atlanta?" *Did you see me and Landon kissing?*

Clint shrugged. He wasn't normally any more or less moody than one would expect a sixteen year old boy to be. But something was on his mind. "You need to talk about anything?"

Clint looked at Jay straight on, studied him, then shrugged again. Jay gritted his teeth, knowing then how Bethany must have felt all those years when shrugs were Jay's favorite response to questions. But Jay shrugged because he honestly hadn't thought anything was going on; Clint had something tumbling around that busy brain of his.

"You know, if you do. If you have any questions."

"Maybe later," Clint said, full of meaning. Jay swallowed thickly. He felt a heavy weight settle in his chest. If Clint knew something, he obviously needed to work it out for himself. That scared the shit out of Jay. He hoped he wasn't right, but only time would tell.

"Night, then. Don't stay up too late."

"Night, Dad."

Jay shut Clint's door behind him, letting out a shaky breath. The look he'd gotten from Clint was similar to, if not a bit kinder, than ones he'd noticed from Ms. Lynne lately. He hoped they were speculative, rather than knowing looks, because even if he was pretty sure what he himself knew now, he wasn't a hundred percent. And how could he answer questions he didn't know how to answer for himself?

It was too soon to know now, right? A couple months friendship had morphed into an unexpected affair with a man for the first time. Even if he realized he obviously had feelings like that for another man, didn't mean he was strictly dickly all of a sudden.

Speaking of.

He went downstairs and found Bethany sitting on the sofa, going through her cell phone. She looked up at his entrance. "Hey, you. Sorry I ended up here so late. I can probably go to my folks' house." She tensed, probably expecting another rude comment like the one that'd slipped out of his mouth when she'd been making herself comfortable in his house earlier.

Not for the first time, he realized, the part of his life that included Bethany as a day-to-day part of his life—aside from as the mother of his children—appeared to well and truly have started feeling like a chapter almost closed. Maybe her being here, helping him come to that realization, hadn't been a bad thing. He did have a flicker of sadness at the thought, but really, he knew what being happy felt like. And what they had, had never truly been that.

"No. You can crash in the guest room if you like."

Her shoulders dropped a fraction, relieved and not disappointed, he hoped. "Thanks, Jay. I finished the dishes."

"Thanks, Beths." He smiled and walked around to take a seat on the sofa beside her. "How are you doing?"

"I'm well. A lot going on right now with work and such." She eyed him. "You seem to be doing well. You seem different." He tried his best to keep from tensing. Was he really that transparent? Or had he been more miserable than he'd known?

"I'm good. Work's going well," he tried for a neutral

151

subject. Bethany looked out the corner of her eye and he knew he wasn't getting off that easily.

"Are you seeing anybody?"

What the hell? Why was everyone so suspicious all of a sudden? Of course, he could just be feeling the pressure of being secretive for the first real time in his life. He didn't like it one bit.

He also didn't like lying. Especially to Bethany. Even if their relationship hadn't been the best for them, he still cared for her. She'd been his friend for such a very long time.

"It's complicated," he answered. Her eyes snapped to his, but a smile crossed her face.

"That's really good. Not the complicated. But that you're seeing someone. If she can get you smiling like that, I should shake her hand."

Jay grunted, a little surprised at her being so supportive. He wasn't so egotistical as to think she still had thoughts of reconciling. Hell, they'd shared dating horror stories enough over the last couple years since their official separation. She'd even seen someone fairly seriously for a couple months.

"What about you?"

She shook her head. "Not so much. But, I'm thinking of making a move soon, so I haven't really been looking. I want to talk to you about it, what it'll mean for the kids, but I want to get my ducks in a row first."

Jay frowned thoughtfully. "Oh-kay," he drawled.

"I should know more come thanksgiving."

"Well, that's only three weeks from now. I suppose the suspense won't kill me," Jay teased. She cast him an unfathomable look, then shook her head and smiled fondly.

She patted his knee. "I'm going to head up to bed. I'll do breakfast in the morning, so you can sleep in, then I'll head out and go see my parents before I head back to Atlanta."

"Sleep good, Beths," he said as she stood to leave.

"You too, Jay. And really. Whatever you're doing, keep doing it. I hate..." She paused, closing her eyes, and sighed. "No would've, should've, could'ves. Just glad you're happy."

"Are you?" he asked.

"I think so," she answered.

And as she walked up the stairs, watching her back, he realized the chapter closed right then. He didn't know what that meant for the next chapter any more than it had before, but this one was well and surely written, crossed, dotted, and the page had turned.

He wasn't surprised at all that his first thought was to call Landon and tell him this development. But to be fair to Landon, himself, and his kids—hell, even to Beths—he had to find the first words for that next chapter, or at least stop holding himself back. So, instead, he surprised himself and called the messenger service to make an appointment with the counselor. If it was time to really be New Jay, or at least the Real Jay, he'd have to do some things that may be a little uncomfortable to Old Jay.

Chapter 16

Landon bounded into the office at the saw mill, a pep in his step. The day had qualified as one of his longest in a while, and his body teetered on the edge of exhaustion. He couldn't give in, excited energy propelled him on. Ms. Lynne, thankfully, had already headed out for the night, since he was coming in later than usual. He signed his mileage log and dropped it in the bin with the rest.

On his way in from his one and only haul for the day, his phone had trilled with two calls he'd been waiting for. He hadn't expected one so soon, and hoped for the other for days. First, the reason he'd taken the morning off, a job proposal from a friend; second, he'd heard from Jay, privately, for the first time in the three days since he'd left Jay's house upon his kids' return.

He felt relief his dad also appeared to have gone for the evening. The only office still occupied was Jay's. Landon knew he probably wagged from head to toe like a dog, but he hadn't even managed to run into the man for more than five minutes in the office.

Jay looked up, beaming when he noticed Landon. Landon's heart gave a pitter patter and he felt entirely too happy to bother with doubts or worries. The man was as obviously happy to see him, so he'd take it.

"Hey," Jay said with a grin, standing up from his chair and coming around the other side of the desk. He paused to look behind Landon, who grabbed him and gave assurances they were alone. Jay reached behind him and slammed the door before their mouths came together. They didn't kiss for long, but they definitely made it count, hot and hard.

"Dang, I missed this," Jay said. Landon's surprise at the statement didn't have time to show before they were kissing again, tongues sliding into each other's mouths. They grappled for one another, clinging almost. Landon's cock grew instantly hard and ready.

Which is why he had to step back. "Well, we definitely can't do this here," Landon said, gasping.

"I know. I know." Jay stepped back himself, straightening his flannel button-down. Landon let himself reach out to straighten Jay's mussed hair where Landon had run his fingers through it. They smiled dopily at one another. "My kids are at their grandparents for church and dinner tonight."

Landon felt his brow furrow. By Jay's own admission, they'd not raised the kids in the church. Jay waved him off. "Some family fellowship thing. Beverly pulled some guilt card when Bethany was home, so the kids agreed to go with them for this shindig. There's a hayride or something."

"Wholesome," Landon teased. Hayrides were a pretty standard fall activity, mostly by local churches during the Halloween season to keep kids from giving in to the wickedness of playing on the Devil's Holiday.

"I have to see you," Jay said, his voice husky and hopeful. Landon would sure take this over the self-recriminations he'd been waiting Jay to start with once his kids came home.

Landon didn't let Jay dwell. "Mine or yours?"

"Yours, okay?"

"Hell, yes. Mine's closer." Landon winked. Also, he wouldn't be watching over his shoulder for the kids to come home early, like last time.

"Meet you there?"

"Absolutely. Let me go get hitched to the trailer for the morning. See you in thirty?"

Jay nodded and quickly went back to whatever work he'd been focused on when Landon came in. Landon's hard-on only wavered when he worked on connecting brake lights and locking the trailer in. The drive home, though, the final spurt of adrenaline from his good afternoon and thoughts of Jay coming over to be in his bed had Landon's pants tented even as he unlocked his front door.

He made quick work of a shower, resisting the urge to stroke himself other than to build his need. He'd barely made it down the stairs in just a pair of old sweatpants when Jay knocked on the front door. Landon practically yanked the man in. Their mouths collided. Jay grunted and laughed into the kiss.

"You taste so good," Landon said, then licked into Jay's mouth again. His hand slid to Jay's straining, denim encased erection. Jay hissed and slid his arms around Landon's waist, dipping into the sweats to palm Landon's ass.

Landon pulled Jay further into the house where they collapsed on the couch. "We should talk," Jay said.

Landon pulled back. "Now?"

Jay laughed, and the sound sent thrills of joy through Landon. "I suppose it can wait."

Landon's head fell back as Jay dropped to the floor and yanked off Landon's pants, sucking him in. "Motherfucker," Landon yelped. Eager, horny Jay was a force to be reckoned with. Landon didn't know what had come over the man, but he sure wouldn't complain.

Jay sucked Landon inexpertly, but enthusiastically. Landon bucked up into his mouth as Jay fondled his balls and hummed. "Damn, Jay. I'm… I'm so fucking close." And wasn't that the damnedest thing. The man got him going like nobody else. Jay looked up through his lashes, full of mischief, then started using his free hand to stroke as he sucked. Landon's incoherent babbling as he shot into Jay's mouth would have been embarrassing were he capable of any kind of thought.

Jay suddenly was in Landon's face, kissing him, letting Landon taste himself on Jay's tongue. God, the taste of his cum in Jay's mouth nearly got him hard again. The clanking of metal as Jay undid his belt and undid his fly, pulled Landon from his stupor. They both laughed as Jay slipped clumsily, while they pushed his jeans down to free his cock and balls.

Landon grasped Jay's cock and didn't even have time to offer a blowjob before Jay howled, dropped his forehead to Landon's, and was spurting over Landon's bare cock and legs.

Their mouths met again, tongues tangling lazily and sweetly as their labored breathing began to settle.

"Fuck me, Landon."

"Apparently, we didn't make that consideration."

Jay put his cheek to Landon's and they lay catching their breath. "That was wild," Jay said. "I swear you make me cum like a damn kid. I can't even last five minutes with you." Jay sounded mildly embarrassed by the fact.

"Fucking-A, Jay. That's the best compliment ever. And in case you didn't notice, I'm not a whole lot better off."

Jay rolled off Landon with a contented sigh, tucking himself away before sitting down on the floor, leaning his back against the couch. Landon put himself to rights as well and swung his legs over the side of the couch, then went to grab each of them a water. Jay took his, casting a lazy grin Landon's way.

"So, how are you?"

"Now he wants to talk, when I can't breathe," Jay said in his most put-upon tone.

Landon playfully nudged the back of Jay's head with his elbow.

When Jay turned a look full of affection and warmth on Landon, he really had to contain himself. "I'm good. Real good."

"What does that mean?" Landon asked.

"Just that I'm good." Jay drank from his water before clearing his throat and turning bashfully away. "I, um, went to see that counselor we used. In Starkville. It's been helpful. We talked on the phone earlier today before I called you, too."

Well, the man was just full of surprises. "I'm glad you say it's helpful."

Jay turned toward Landon. "I just wanted to say thank you, because you've been really patient with me."

"Oh." Landon gave Jay a kiss on the temple, feeling a little silly, but happy Jay only ducked his head and hid a shy grin at the action. "Of course, Jay. This was never meant to be any pressure. It could be two guys who are convenient in this one horse town. Or whatever." *Liar.*

Jay fell silent, like he didn't know what to say to that any more than Landon. *Too soon. Don't push.* Landon told himself. Hell, he hadn't even told Mitch about their little

160

affair, because he didn't need anyone else to tell him how badly this could all turn out. But surely, Jay was coming out of his shell and making strides. Landon could give it a little more time.

"Jay, this isn't something you have to prove to me. You just get right with you, okay. Figure out what to do for *you* for once, something you can live with for *you* and for your kids. Don't think about me, or about Bethany, or what folks will think. It's hard, being raised around here. But this is big." Landon ran his fingers through Jay's hair, lightly massaging his scalp, enjoying how Jay leaned into the touch.

"You're too good to me, Landon."

"I know," he said. Jay reached up and gave him a gentle shove. They fell silent again. The afterglow was too nice, and the companionable moment was just that. There was no recrimination, and Landon meant it fully when he meant he was Jay's friend here, as well as his lover. Even if his heart was in it deeper than he'd intended, Jay hadn't asked any more than Landon could give, hadn't played games with him. The mutual respect he felt, made all the difference to Landon. If they went their separate ways, or just ended up friends, he'd be very sad, but wouldn't be bitter. Jay was no user, not telling Landon pretty words like some selfish prick.

Jay started randomly humming a song as Landon rubbed his scalp. It was amazing how quickly the sound of the man's gentle, deep voice quieted Landon's thoughts. The long day caught up with Landon, the calm of the moment settling in his bones, and with a smile, he drifted off to sleep on his couch.

Chapter 17

"You know you were kind of a jerk," Brittany said.

"I know, I know. I thought you slept with my crush, though," Landon replied, readjusting the phone on his shoulder as he reached for a box of instant oatmeal to put in his basket.

"Well, you know, heterosexual men tend to sleep with women, so being a jealous basket case every time he flirts with someone isn't quite the way to handle the straight-boy crush."

Landon grimaced. He still didn't know whether he should say anything about that to his friends. He wasn't much up for the lecture, nor was it his business to out the man, even to people Jay may never see again.

"Please tell me you're not a dick around the ex-wife."

Again, Landon grimaced. "Landon!" Brittany scolded. "You need to get it together, sweetie. Seriously, you can't go around acting like a raging, jealous queen. Even if by some miracle you did start sleeping with him, his ex is a sacred thing, you know. They have kids."

"I know that, B. Seriously. I wasn't necessarily a

dick. I just thought bad thoughts."

"Honey, haven't we all."

"Anyway," Landon said with a huff. "I just wanted to clear the air. I felt bad I was such a jerk."

"Oh, it's understandable. For the record, I so would have hit that."

"Oh, I saw your patented head tilt and Bambi eyes routine."

"My best moves!" she whined. Landon laughed. Damn, he loved his friends.

"Okay, hon, I've got to get off here and finish my grocery shopping."

"Helluva Friday. You're such a party animal."

"You're tellin' me," Landon scoffed. They ended their call with promises to get in touch soon. He'd promised Mitch he'd try to make it down during Thanksgiving holidays when he had a few days off in a row.

He peered wistfully at his phone, wishing Jay would call, but knowing that wouldn't happen. He still hadn't managed to tell Jay about his job offer. In the couple of days since he had fallen asleep to Jay's humming, they'd only seen one another at work. And Landon wasn't ready to share the news with his dad until he knew for sure he'd be taking the position, so the time hadn't presented itself. They'd attempted to make plans for the weekend, but Bethany had some surprise news she'd come down for the weekend to share.

Landon didn't begrudge her that. After that initial shock of Bethany making herself at home, Landon had truly come to grips with the fact that she would always be the mother of Jay's kids. Whether he and Jay were ever actually together or just remained friends, she'd be around in some capacity. Though, he didn't hate it that she lived hundreds of miles away for now.

Landon came out of the tiny frozen food aisle of their small country grocery store and ran into some familiar faces.

"Hey, Mr. Landon!" Millie waved at him when she and Clint saw him. They'd seen each other once more since they got home after stopping by the saw mill to get something from their daddy. The kids were always unfailingly polite, but Clint seemed to study Landon every time. Millie, though, was always ready with a smile and a hello.

Landon stopped and gave them a hello. They looked so much like their daddy, it made Landon's stomach knot up. They both had those same kind brown eyes and light brown hair. Clint was almost the spitting image of a younger Jay, while Millie had her mother's chin and nose.

"Thought y'all had company tonight?" How else did one make small talk with kids, especially ones whose father you were carrying on with?

"Oh, yeah, Dad sent us for dessert," Clint mumbled, definitely uncomfortable.

KADE BOEHME

Millie beamed, though. "They sent us out because they have to talk about mother coming back home!"

Landon gawped. He noticed a flush crawl up Clint's face as he shushed his sister. "What?" she snapped at her brother, then turned a smile back on Landon. "After grandmama and grandpa left, mother said she was moving back." Landon's stomach lurched.

"They said they were going to discuss it," Clint mumbled. Landon blinked, forcing his expression to something close to good cheer.

"Well, that's good news." News Jay surely hadn't expected, and news Landon would fucking *love* to flail over. But not in front of the kids. Millie's mood reflected such joy, he couldn't be angry. And surely Bethany didn't intend *home* to be Jay's. Could he even get angry over that, if she was? They had years of history, and at best, they'd determined Jay was bisexual. There hadn't been any labels attached at all so far, and he'd obviously been happy with her for a time. They had seventeen years and two children.

"Uh, we should probably get home," Clint mumbled, giving his sister a push.

"Oh. Yeah," Landon said lamely, then smiled and nodded at them both. "Y'all have a good night." He definitely wasn't going to send his best to their folks because Lord knows that could come across as passive aggressive.

Hell, he was too surprised to even be actually aggressive, much less something as calculated as passive aggressive. He'd learned Jay could be surprising, though.

He'd trusted him so far. Even if they were going to end this…

Who was he kidding? After he paid out, he didn't know why, but the tension, the strain of it all, hit him. He definitely didn't want to push, but he had to ask, or at least stake some sort of small claim. If Bethany might be back for keeps, he had to at least let Jay know to think about him.

He made his way to his truck, then dropped his head on the steering wheel. He'd known this day might come, even if he hadn't quite seen this. And he owed it to Jay to let him figure out what he wanted to do. Hell, he was guessing wildly, anyways, off the word of a twelve year old girl who didn't know much more factually than Landon did himself.

He straightened in his seat, turned over the ignition, and headed for home. He didn't know how to handle this. He had the feeling all he could do was wait. Even if that was hard as hell. He had to trust Jay.

***

Jay's night had started out surprising, why shouldn't it end with a bigger bang? That seemed to be the theme of his life over the last several months.

Bethany's call earlier in the day announcing she would be coming in from Atlanta in the afternoon surprised only Jay and the kids, it appeared. When her parents arrived before her, they apparently had known the visit was planned. Premeditated surprises like this evening were some of Jay's least favorite things because in Bethany's case, it usually did lead to bigger things.

Her sharp gaze had searched him out the whole night since she'd gotten there. He really had been at a loss. She'd seemed almost accusatory, pointed comments slipping into conversation here and there.

Bethany's father watching them, spoke of a man who didn't know what his daughter or wife were about any more than Jay. But her mother, Beverly, cast a shrewd look his way every now and then.

They'd left after hushed conversation in the living room, the kids and Jay all shrugged at each other while waiting for Bethany to return.

Then Bethany had lowered the boom. "Remember I had some news?" She gazed at Jay first, then turned to give each of the kids a grin. "I got a job in Winona. I'm moving home!"

Millie'd bounced from her chair, squealing happily, while Clint flicked his surprised gaze between both his parents. Jay felt gobsmacked. Not that he was angry with her for getting a job closer to the kids. He knew they'd missed her. But a job so close to his home? He hoped she didn't mean… surely not.

Since it wasn't late in the night, not much past seven p.m., he'd offered Clint the keys to his truck and sent them the fifteen minutes to Kilmichael with a "Me and your mom need to discuss some things." Millie's expression had been baleful at best, but Clint had quickly scuttled her out the door.

The door barely closed behind them before Bethany

snapped. "I figured you'd be happy for us."

He put his hands up. "I'm absolutely happy for you. A little warning would have been nice."

"I didn't know my life required your signing off on decisions anymore."

He left his hands up, still surprised at the heat in her tone. "Seriously, Beths, I'm not mad. I'm surprised as hell. And you're all too right. I don't have a say. This is just gonna be a big deal. We didn't discuss how it'd work with living arrangements and such."

She straightened. "That depends."

"Depends?"

"Mama got to talking with Lynne Sutherland at the auction last weekend."

Jay had to bite his tongue to hold in his groan. "I can only imagine what she had to say."

"I already had this job lined up. But Jay, so help me, if you're really fucking Landon Petty, I can only imagine you've lost your damned mind, and my coming home is happening just in time."

Jay felt the world tilt under his feet. "I…" *Say something, damn it.* Even if he'd feared this might be what she was talking about, he hadn't expected her to blurt it out like that. And he also hadn't expected the vitriol. She was much more level headed that this, and he'd not known her to ever have a hateful bone in her body.

"Beths. What the hell?"

"Tell me, Jay. Are you fucking a man?"

"What the hell does that have to do with anything?" Stupid question, of course. He probably should have guessed it might be a big deal. She may have lived in a big city, but maybe the small town girl wasn't ready for this kind of revelation.

"Do you know how goddamned embarrassing this would be, Jay? Is this why you didn't fight for us at all?"

"What? Bethany. I…" He rubbed his hand over his face. "I've been working this out with a counselor."

"Oh, that's fucking rich. You'll get your shit together for a *man*? Are you kidding?"

"No! What are you saying? You know me better. I'm not doing this for anyone. I'm thinking about *me*."

"Exactly," she snapped, pointing a finger in his face. He'd never seen her so angry, so damned hurt. He wished he could do something, but she had him dead to rights. He couldn't exactly lie, could he?

"Do you know what this could do to the kids?" She asked, tears starting to fall. He dared not reach for her. He felt as lost as he ever had. And fuck if he didn't want Landon right then. Which made him close his eyes and sigh.

"I don't understand, Beths. You think this is hard for you? Imagine me? I didn't *know* something about myself that was this important."

"Your mama knew. She was always telling me to be a better wife, to buck up and not worry you so much."

Jay couldn't help barking a bitter laugh. "Funny, she said that same shit to me. And you know what? It made me learn to never worry anyone with anything, to keep people from worrying about me, I just shut it down."

"Well, I'm so glad you're finally letting it all out," she snarked.

Jay deflated. He remembered his counselor saying if he intended to have this conversation, it'd be worse if done during an argument. But how could he fix that if that'd been how the whole damn conversation started. He didn't know why the world had gone mad all of a sudden, but he wished Lynne Fucking Sutherland had kept her goddamned mouth shut.

"This is not the Jay I know."

He looked at her, sadly. "And this isn't the Bethany I know. You're my friend, the one I've known forever. You don't do shit like this."

"And *you* don't fuck men!"

"Bethany!"

Before the argument could go any further, headlights shone through the front windows. Jay looked at Bethany steadily. "Do we do this in front of them? Do you tell them *for* me or do I get a chance to speak to them?"

"You're going to *tell them*?"

"Won't they wonder, Beths? Won't they want to know why you suddenly don't want them in my life?" His voice shook on the last word and she paused. She sobbed, clenching her fist.

"Jay, I don't know what to do here. But I promise, I can't let this stand." The fear that struck in Jay's heart at that moment, at the anger and recrimination in her voice. He hurt, deep down. He knew she was surprised. He supposed he was still getting used to the idea of being into men, regardless of what that made him, so she had the right to freak out. But this was making his head hurt and his heart ache.

"I'm going to bed. I'll stay here tonight and let you say your peace, but tomorrow, I'm leaving with my kids."

He wanted to toss her out, lock her out. She couldn't do this. How could the first time he'd felt right in his whole life be about to cost him so damn much?

The kids came in, thankfully laughing. Jay looked up to where their mother had disappeared upstairs. There was no way they could miss his too bright eyes or his heated face. "Are you two fighting again?" Millie's face clouded. God, but he hated making so many people he loved unhappy in less than one horrible hour.

Jay couldn't stand it anymore, and collapsed in the recliner. "Sit down, guys. We need to talk."

Chapter 18

Millie's stormy expression was so unusual. Of the whole family, she was always sunshine and light. He couldn't believe he was having this conversation, but at the same time, he felt oddly ready to just get it off his chest—at least to these two people, the ones who meant the most to him in the world.

He'd do whatever he could to make them happy, to keep them healthy. If that meant leaving with their mother in the morning, what could he say? They lived in Mississippi. Montgomery County, at that. Mothers always got the kids, it was just a fact. And that he had admitted to being with a man, he didn't even know the implications. He'd been in a homosexual relationship for five whole minutes, so he hadn't quite wrapped his head around the new politics that would come with that life.

"I'm going to have a conversation with you guys that you might not like."

"You didn't tell mother to stay in Atlanta, did you?" Millie asked. He scowled at her petulance.

"You're twelve years old, Millie, I need you to act like it for a little while here." Millie stared at her father, not one for being stern all that often. She nodded. Clint's gaze was steady on Jay, though. He didn't appear surprised they were about to have whatever conversation they were going to have.

"Y'all are old enough, I feel I can talk to you for real."

They nodded solemnly, Millie looking a little wary.

"Now, you know your mama and I were never going to get back together. We told you when we split up, it was nothing to do with y'all, we just … We didn't work." More nods. "Millie, when your mama said she was coming home, she meant she'd probably live with your grandparents or in Winona. Which you know is a lot closer, only thirty minutes. But she isn't going to live here."

"I know that, daddy." She said, seriously. He studied her carefully, noticing just how much she'd grown. She was, for all intents and purposes, a young lady now. Didn't mean the news was going to be taken easily, but at least he wasn't about to try to explain this to a six year old. He didn't know if he'd have been able to handle this if they'd been any younger.

Hell, he didn't know if he could handle it now. Again, he found himself wishing he had Landon here, but that wouldn't be fair. He hadn't even told Landon what he wanted. He was entirely too wrung out to think on that right then, so, much like Old Jay, he tucked that away until the task at hand was completed.

"Millie, you know how when me and mom separated, we didn't want you to be uncomfortable, or to feel like you were keeping secrets, but that the divorce was a grown-up thing?"

"Spit it out, Dad," Clint said.

Jay slumped. "You guys can tell who you want. I'm not going to make you keep secrets. It's not my place. If you need to talk to someone, I won't stop you." Clint and Millie shared a long look. "I've been figuring out some things, talking to a professional, and all." Jay didn't imagine there was an easier way to say it. "I've been seeing someone."

"Mr. Petty," Clint said, expression open. Jay's eyes flicked between the kids. Millie seemed startled by the news, but neither of them looked angry.

"How?"

"I saw you guys." Clint's face went scarlet at his admission.

"You did?" Millie asked, clearly grossed out.

"When you came home last week?"

"Ew, daddy!" Millie said. "That's why you were out in the dark?"

"No," Clint said, quietly. "I went to the office before we went to Atlanta and the door was open and you guys were… making out."

Jay closed his eyes, feeling his own face flush. "Oh, son, I'm sorry… I know it must have been a surprise."

"Not that it was a man…" Clint rolled his eyes. "Okay, I did freak out about that, but we were away all that week and I realized mostly I was freaked to see my dad making out with anyone."

"Gross," Millie stated again. Her nose scrunched up. "A man, daddy? People are gonna be such jerks about this. I can't believe you're gay."

Clint grimaced. "Are you?"

Jay had to be honest. "I don't know that I'm completely gay. I did care very much for your mother. I still do, in my own way. But I also have been seeing Landon, and I think I'm getting to be okay with that. But your mom is having a hard time with it. Which is absolutely not her fault. I understand if you guys do, too."

"I don't know, dad. This is gonna suck so bad," Millie said, a tear falling.

Clint looked at Millie in that superior way teenagers tend to look at those they deem less intelligent than them. "It wouldn't if you kept you mouth shut."

Before they could start sniping, Jay held a hand up and tiredly replied. "If Millie needs to talk to people to work it out for herself, we can't get in her way." Although a childish part inside him wanted to insist she leave grown-up business to grown-ups.

"I want to talk to mom," she said, shakily. Jay smiled sadly at her, wishing he could make it better for her. But what could he say? He'd been dealing with this a short time, but in that short time, in his time being so damn happy with Landon, he'd tried to make all the right steps, do the right thing. And now, the right thing was not lying. Because this was not just going to go away.

He perked up a bit when that thought crossed his mind. Regardless of how he labeled this, he could no sooner have stopped himself being attracted to Landon than he could have Bethany. He cared for Landon, that wasn't something he'd chosen. He couldn't change it, and he didn't want to.

"She's in the guest room." When Millie stood to leave, he held out a hand. "I love you, Millie. So much." She didn't say anything to that, but she did hug him quickly before running upstairs.

The quiet was strange after Millie left. Not necessarily strained, but not comfortable. Both Jay and Clint were lost in thought. His son didn't seem to be losing his mind over the news, but he'd had time to work through it, which neither Bethany nor Millie had.

"You smile more," Clint said.

"What?" Jay glanced Clint's direction. Again, he marveled at how old his kids had gotten. Clint was practically a man. Hell, he was just shy of Jay's height at this point.

"You smile more. I wondered if maybe you were dating someone. My friends always seemed dumber when they were getting laid."

"Clint!"

"What?" Clint's crooked grin brought a levity that Jay felt guilty, but grateful to accept. "You know my boy Zach was. Well, is."

Jay started. "Zach Cummings?" They'd grown up together, Zach and Clint. They did everything together for a long while, but that had stopped at some point Jay had to admit he didn't remember.

"He, um, kissed me." Again, Clint's face turned scarlet.

"Oh?" Jay tried to keep his tone neutral.

"Yeah. I was a dick after that. Guys at school gave him shit after I stopped hanging out with him. I didn't apologize 'til right before we moved." Clint looked at his dad, distraught. Jay couldn't bring himself to scold his son for the language when he looked like that. "And he forgave me. For no reason. Then when I saw you and I called him, he told me not to be a dick to you like I was to him."

Jay wanted to drive to Columbus right then and offer to pay the kid's college tuition.

"Dad, it's weird as hell. I won't lie. But I do love you."

Jay couldn't stop himself from moving quickly across the room and hugging his son. Clint patted Jay's back awkwardly and he moved back, clearing his throat. "Sorry," Jay said. Then he hugged Clint again. "No, I'm not."

178

Clint laughed.

God. Damn. That was the most beautiful sound he'd heard that night. Jay pulled away and wiped his eyes. Clint patted his dad's shoulder. "You're alright, old man."

Jay shook his head, staring at his son in wonder. "When did you grow up?"

"Dad, don't get weird." Clint smirked. "Weirder."

Jay chuckled, feeling lighter. God, this wasn't over by a very long shot. But Clint's acceptance was a balm on his soul tonight. He was very glad his kids had been born in a different time than him, all of a sudden.

"I'm gonna go talk to the girls," Clint said. "Night, dad."

Jay felt like his bones weighed a thousand pounds. He sank back down into the recliner after Clint went upstairs, and closed his eyes. He just needed a minute. He was so weary, just a minute and he'd shut off the lights and go to bed.

Chapter 19

Jay felt like he'd just blinked and suddenly the early morning sun was peeking in the front windows, shining in his face. He jerked awake, realizing he'd slept on the damn recliner. He'd scolded himself for a moment for not having done the dishes, but when the events of the night before crashed down on him, he suddenly didn't give two shits.

At least the chores now would occupy his mind until he knew what to do next. The world felt new and scary. Again.

Part of him wished things would quit changing so fast, but another, bigger part of him couldn't deny that while things were big and horrible, his shoulders had this crazy amount of weight off he hadn't even realized he'd been carrying.

He made his way to the kitchen and set up the coffee maker, then got to working on cleaning the dishes from the night before; he loaded some in the dishwasher and soaked pots and pans in the sink. The mess of a world gone insane littered his counters, even down to the melted tub of ice cream they'd never finished that sat on the coffee table in the living room.

He'd just dropped a detergent pod in the dishwasher and

flicked it on when the sound of the front door swishing open caught his attention. His heart thudded happily for a moment, wondering if it would be Landon. *Shit! Landon.*

Pulling his phone out of his pocket, he noted not only that it was just barely after eight a.m., but also that Landon tried to call the night before. The quiet clearing of a throat drew Jay's attention back to the living room, to where Bethany had just come in. She wore pink sweatpants that actually said PINK and an off the shoulder sweatshirt. Her dirty blond hair was up in a ponytail, and she still wore the makeup she'd been wearing the night before, though it was definitely more smudged.

"Hi," she said, quietly.

"Hey."

They stood, awkwardly looking around, not speaking for a while. The coffee pot beeped to signal it'd finished brewing. They silently did their ages old morning routine, but it felt all wrong. Not because of the anger and the fight they'd had, but because this was not her home and this was no longer their lives. The place she occupied now should be Landon's. He hadn't even told the man.

"Look, Jay…" She stopped, leaned against the counter, and stared down into her coffee. He smelled cigarette smoke coming off her clothes. She hadn't smoked in years, save for a few deaths in the family and the day their divorce was finalized. Unless she'd picked it up in her eighteen months in Atlanta. Those little things one used to know about a person seemed to fade away when your lives went in opposite directions.

"You really have been talking to the counselor about this, huh?"

"Yes." Jay was honestly talked out, but this was important. He could do it. He *had* to do it. "Right after… well, after I started seeing Landon as more than a friend, I decided I needed to understand how I'd shut that part of me off for so long."

"I guess I just don't understand."

"I didn't either, at first. Honestly. Until I thought back on the few close guy friends I had over the years and realized, like you said, my mama did get it and she held my daddy's worrying over me so much. I guess I just… blocked out anything that might make it worse."

Her sadness was palpable when she asked "We never worked, did we?"

"I don't know how to answer that." But suddenly a truth spilled from him, "And I don't know if it's because Landon is a man, or if it's because it's him… I'm truly happy." The admission, though he hated seeing how much it hurt her, was a moment of clarity for him. "I can't say it's not just because I finally know all of me, be that bisexual or one of the crazy words my counselor says describes all the different sexualities…"

"I'm a nurse practitioner, Jay. I've heard most of it at some point." Her dry tone made Jay grit his teeth.

"Then, even if you don't understand, you should have some professional knowledge that I didn't *pick* this."

Her posture went rigid, but she quickly deflated. "That doesn't make it easier, Jay. It just doesn't. I get it. I've taken psych classes, I work with tons of gay male nurses. But you're thirty-six. It's hard to get, you just... never cared."

"I can't go back through our entire divorce and all those things I didn't even know were wrong. I don't see, now, how it makes a difference. We've been apart emotionally and sexually for almost five years. I understood when you said you needed more. We'd both given as much as we could to each other. But who's to say, if you hadn't gotten pregnant, or we'd actually gone separate ways during college, I wouldn't have found out sooner. But we can't play the what if game anymore. The time for that was over when the ink dried a year and a half ago, longer if you count when you moved out three years ago."

Her startled gaze met Jay's. "You really did get all in touch with your inner self, huh?"

"Yeah," Jay grumbled. "I'm still trying to figure out how I feel about him. But I like him a lot more than I liked the old me. Ignorant me is hard to think back on when I'm so happy."

Bethany sighed. "I said cruel things last night."

"You did," Jay replied evenly.

"I was surprised."

"I can respect that. Doesn't mean I have to forgive some of it any time soon."

Bethany smirked. "A gay good ole boy. How does that work?"

"I don't think, no matter how simple I felt at times, I was ever just your average redneck, Beths."

"You're right. You always were kinder than the guys we grew up with. It's one thing I liked so much about you." She tapped her fingers on her coffee cup. "I feel like the shitty ex-wife who flew through in hysterics, making things bad, but Jay, this is a tough road to hoe. And I won't lie, even I'm gonna take some adjusting."

"I happen to know a good counselor."

She snorted. "Idiot."

"Maybe it wouldn't be so bad for Millie to go, Clint if he wants."

She nodded. "Millie probably. She's confused, but she's just a little girl. She doesn't have any point of reference. A lot like you, I suppose."

"You'd be surprised what meeting one openly gay person did to my poor little brain."

She frowned. "Maybe if you had long ago."

"I don't know," Jay said. "I feel like I'm old enough now, I know life is do or die. Any younger and I might have been more likely to keep shoving it back. Maybe it was just the right person at the right time."

She held up her hand. "I'm really not ready to talk about that. I'm sorry Jay, I'm just not." She looked a bit baffled. "But when did Clint grow up? He just came in and made so much sense. Then I felt like the biggest heel that my own kids can at least roll with the punches and I'm shrieking like a soap opera villain."

"You were surprised," Jay reiterated charitably. He held his breath after he asked if she really intended to take the kids.

"Will you at least discuss with me before you introduce them to Landon as anything... more? And I mean if either of them is so uncomfortable they prefer living with me, I'll not fight you, I'll just say 'okay.'"

Jay nodded slowly. "I can live with that."

She started crying, but Jay didn't reach for her. It wasn't his place, and she didn't seem to want him to anyway. After she wept for a while, she announced she'd go shower, then she and the kids were going to spend the day together.

"Jay? I need to not talk to you for a while, okay? Unless it's about the kids." She seemed on the edge of losing it, again, and Jay couldn't tell whether it would be anger or tears, or a nasty storm of the two. He quietly watched her go.

Clint sauntered into the kitchen, fully primped and dressed, while Jay poured himself another coffee. "You're dressed and ready awful early," Jay said.

Clint grunted and made his way for his own coffee cup. "I promised mom and Millie we could go to Council House over in French Camp for breakfast. On me."

Jay scoffed. "On me, then"

Clint gave a toothy, sarcastic grin. "Pretty much."

"You can use the truck if you won't all fit in yours." That Clint's old Toyota pickup was too small was a given.

"Thanks, dad. Oh, hey, did you talk to Landon? Millie and her big mouth. We saw him at the store. She told him mom was moving home and I couldn't really say anything in front of her. But I'm assuming with your big gay coming out you, uh, might wanna let him know … whatever." Clint's words fell out, but Jay caught them. Horror flashed through him as he remembered Landon *had* called last night while he and Bethany fought. It was awkward acting like a teenager in front of, well, his teenager, but he freaked out right there.

"Shit."

"Yeah," Clint said, at least a little sympathetically. "Um, before you… He's not going to be like coming for dinners and shit yet, is he? I'm thinking that's... too soon."

"First, language, second, no. I wouldn't even do that if I'd only been dating a woman for a couple months." *That's the party line, anyway.* But he did understand. Jay wasn't sure *he* was ready for the kids to know Landon was there as his date yet.

Clint eyed his dad skeptically and sipped his coffee.

Jay checked his phone again, noting Landon hadn't left a voicemail. But while they'd been talking, a call had come in from the office phone. He wanted to pull his hair out, knowing he needed to talk to Landon and tell him the new developments, even that he realized Landon had fit into his life while Jay hadn't been paying attention.

He wanted to sit in the comfort of Landon's company and make better promises than he'd been able to make before. Because truth be told, he'd known it had become more real than he'd expected, probably when they'd made love—er, with penetration—the first time; but it'd definitely become real when they'd sat quietly with Landon running his fingers through Jay's hair, Jay humming in the quiet night. He'd never felt peace like that, not since he held his children in his arms the first time, and something close to it at fifteen when a pretty girl named Beth sat down and asked him why he was so quiet.

He dialed the office first, hoping this would be quick. "Jay, son, good mornin' to ya. Sorry to call so early."

"It's okay, Ricky. What's going on?"

"I honestly didn't realize it was s'early. It wasn't that urgent. Just was a little surprised, so I wanted to make sure you were filled in."

"No time like the present." *I suppose.* It was definitely still early, there was time to go to Landon's.

"It's about Landon."

Jay's heart dropped. "What's that?"

"Landon put in his notice. He's leaving, so we're going to have to look for someone new." The old man didn't sound pleased at all, grudging at best.

"I'll be damned."

"Yeah. Boy said he wants to use his degree. Guess I can't be too mad at him. But, I hate to see him go."

Jay sat silent, stunned. Landon was leaving? How was it possible? Surely… not after this. He hadn't even let Jay explain.

"Son, you still there?"

"Um. Yessir. Sorry. Still tired. And it's a bit of a shock."

"I'll say. We'll talk more about it later. Like I said, it wasn't important enough for me to have called so early. Wasn't paying any attention. I'll let you get back to your family. Unless, maybe you need to know… he's at home." Jay balked, but at this point, he wondered who *didn't* know. Ms. Lynne and her fucking mouth.

"Yessir."

"Have a good day."

Jay shouted up the stairs he would be taking Clint's truck, which was met with silence. He opened the door and realized everyone had gone already. That didn't give him pause.He ran to the truck and flew down the road. He almost laughed hysterically realizing he was chasing after someone, and that someone was a man... and he didn't care. New Jay was going to be happy, and New Jay was going to get through this with his family. He just hoped Landon was up for it.

***

Landon stumbled down his stairs, blearily rubbing his eyes. Someone was banging on his fucking front door and Landon's hangover did not appreciate it. At all.

He flung the door open, poised to snap, but Jay stood on the other side looking worse for the wear.

"Um, Jay?"

"You quit?"

"What?" His brain wasn't quite awake yet, so he didn't know what crazy talk the man was speaking about. Jay's shirt and jeans were rumpled and he was barefoot. "You drove here without shoes?"

"You quit the mill?"

What? Oh. "Oh, yeah." He remembered his miserable night last night. He'd told his daddy about his new job after he left the grocery store, mostly to keep from calling Jay a thousand times. His mama had insisted Landon's daddy accept his resignation—one Landon hadn't yet intended to give.

"Jay... Just..." He shook his head, trying to wake up. "Fuck. Come in."

Jay grabbed Landon. "I don't want you to move. I told the kids everything. It's all crazy and everything is tossed up in the air, but I don't want you gone."

Landon blinked.

"Landon, I realized long enough ago I should be ashamed for being so wishy-washy, that you're so right. Just… you're right. And you made all the lights in my head come on. Then I realized, you make me feel so comfortable with myself and I'm alive all of a sudden."

"Jay, are you high?"

Jay scowled. "I'm trying to tell you I'm pretty sure I'm in love with you, more in love than I've ever been, and you think I'm high?" Jay threw his hands up. "I'm fucking this all to hell."

Landon frowned. Jay only used words like that when they were having sex, so the man was frustrated but—Wait.

Landon put his hands on Jay's face and held his head still. "Did you just tell me you came out to your kids and that you think you love me?"

Jay suddenly went all bashful, cheeks getting pink, eyes casting down. And then he met Landon's gaze straight on. "I'm saying I know I am. I love you, Landon."

Landon felt his eyes go wide.

"I kind of thought, especially when I realized for weeks now, you just fit. In my life, in my bed. But I was so caught up in all these new things happening in my head and trying to figure it all out. I wasn't listening to my heart.. But yeah. When your daddy said you resigned, I realized I thought you were hurt because you thought Beth was moving in with me because Clint told me Millie told him and I've never run that fast in my life. I've never want to stop from hurting someone so much, except my kids—but that's a given, they're my—"

Landon shut Jay up with a huge, smiling, laughing kiss. Even his hangover couldn't stop him from wanting to sing like the Hillbilly Sound of Music or something.

"Are you kidding me?"

"No," Jay said, seriously. Landon ran a thumb over Jay's furrowed brows, smoothing the lines there. "I hate how much Beth is hurting over this, and it feels wrong because I don't want to disregard our marriage. I *care* for her. I always have and always will. But Landon, I absolutely fucking love you. And I know it's gonna be hard to deal with and hell, we may not last, but… Hell, I wanna try. I wanna make promises and spend time with you and I don't want you hurt because you're waiting for me to get my shit together."

Jay stopped. "Although, I may just be assuming you want the same thing." He winced.

"Are you crazy?" Jay closed his eyes and Landon pressed forward. "I was scared I'd fallen that weekend we spent together just working on the deck and drinking beer. I knew I probably had the moment you started humming your song to me the other night. I'd never been in for real love, but that moment… I thought it had to be love. But last night, after Millie told me Bethany said she was coming home, I did worry, I had a moment of panic."

He held Jay's face, stroking his thumbs over Jay's cheekbones. Jay's beautiful, soulful brown eyes roamed Landon's face. "But the moment I absolutely knew I could trust you, that you'd be here today, if not tomorrow or the next day, I knew you were mine. I knew then I loved you." And Landon meant every word. He'd realized after he'd talked to his folks and decided to take the job, that he'd been patient, waiting for the right opportunity to finally strike out on his own to come. Jay would come too, with just a bit more patience. He had such faith in the man.

"I thought I'd lost you."

"Nope. I told you I'd wait it out, and I meant it. I believe in you, Jay. You've always been up front with me. So don't doubt me, either."

"I won't." Jay dropped his forehead to Landon's and one, two, three breaths later, the man fucking *sobbed*. And Landon held him as Jay wept. Jay mumbled tearful words of sorrow for hurting people, and guilt for not feeling guilty that he'd wanted Landon. He said words of love and hope in that laughter-through-tears way that made Landon smile and hug the man closer.

Finally, Jay pulled back and looked at Landon with a wet smile. "So, what's this job? Do you have to move?"

"No. It's at that little private school in Starkville. It'll be a bit of a drive, but my friend is the assistant headmaster. She knows about me and while, like us living here, teaching there and being out wouldn't be totally wise, they do have other quietly gay staff, otherwise she'd never have offered."

"That's great. I'm so happy for you."

"I'm not leaving you, Jay. We have time. I start in the winter semester, but I'll still be living right here." Landon paused. "What about your kids? How… how's that?"

Jay sighed and explained a bit about how the night went. Landon wasn't surprised Clint had figured it out, not based on the looks the boy'd given him.

"Oh, Ms. Lynne is a pain in my ass, I tell you," Landon snapped. "But daddy had warned me."

Jay's eyes grew wide. "So he does know."

"I think so, why?"

"Nothing, he's just the one who told me you were here this morning, if I wanted to talk."

Landon chuckled. "I feel like there should be a country song about this."

Jay huffed. "I have the feeling we're not quite there yet."

Landon smiled and pressed a kiss to Jay's mouth. "No, but we're closer every day. Your kids are proof, even if it takes Millie time. Times are a changin'."

"So he says to the former heterosexual."

Landon didn't know why that made him laugh so hard, but it did. They both did, for a long while. Laughed and kissed and just were light and free in the little house in the country.

"Former, eh? Prove it," Landon said, nuzzling Jay's jaw, grinding their cocks together.

"I think I can handle that." Jay let out a quiet moan, one that rolled right through Landon. Then Jay stunned Landon into stillness by whispering "I want you to do me."

Landon met Jay's unguarded gaze, all the feeling there almost undoing him. "What do you—" Before he finished his question, Jay's quirked eyebrow told him he'd been asking a silly question, but he hadn't wanted to assume. "Jay, babe, you don't have to…"

"I *want* to, though. I love how it felt when it was us, together like that. I just… I want you to know I mean all of this, that I'm here in this one hundred percent."

"That doesn't mean you have to let me fuck you, Jay."

Jay grimaced, but still smiled. "Good because I was hoping you'd be gentler than that since it's my first time and all." Jay suddenly looked nervous, but his open, vulnerable expression was steadfast. "I don't wanna just seal it with a kiss. This is important. I want you to make love to me."

"Yeah?" Landon's voice faltered, the gravity of what Jay offered hitting him right in the chest, making butterflies burst in his stomach. The moment felt heavy, important. Perfect. Jay nodded once, then kissed the corner of Landon's mouth and whispered "yeah."

Landon took Jay's hand, took a deep breath, and led him up the stairs and to the bedroom.

Chapter 20

Once upon a time, Jay thought maybe he'd feel less manly, or perhaps more *gay* if he lay with a man like this. Yes, now that he thought back on it, honestly, he could recognize those moments in which he'd thought he might like being taken care of in bed. Those moments had been pushed back, chalked up to being random, fleeting thoughts every man gets in life where he thinks on some sexual taboo to get his dick twitching.

Now, though, with Landon having stripped him slowly and kissed him over every inch, Jay's body buzzed and sung with a need he didn't know he'd had. To be touched, to let go, was a scary-as-hell thing for a split second, but having surrendered to Landon's hands and lips and tongue, Jay almost wept at how deeply he *felt*. His heart pounded and his stomach clenched in pleasure, his breath deepened. Jay felt like he'd come apart and Landon was slowly pulling him open.

Then Landon looked up at him with gentle, loving grin and kissed Jay's bare chest, stroking Jay's cock with one hand and asked "You're sure?"

Part of Jay wanted to say *no, fuck no*. A million moments in their relationship had changed and rearranged Jay's life. Even if he never did this particular act again, he felt it'd be as life changing as the first time Landon had blown him, or the first time he'd taken Landon in his mouth, or the first time he'd fucked Landon.

A twinge of guilt had Jay placing a shaking hand on Landon's face, palm to cheek. "Landon, I don't think less of you because I've done this to you. The topping bit."

Landon's confused expression had Jay pulling him up for a heady kiss then he finished his thought. "Sorry, me and my talking again. I guess, I just feel like this is big. You know." Landon's smirk made Jay roll his eyes in a way that'd make his kids proud. *Not the time to think about them.* "I just mean this, us doing this for the first time… I feel like it's going to make me different."

Landon's brow furrowed in concern. "Jay? We don't have to."

"No!" Jay said, louder than he'd intended, placing both hands on Landon's face, opening his legs wider, wrapping his calves around Landon's thighs. And it felt right, holding Landon like that, having him there.

"I didn't mean that, Landon. I just meant… I'll be different, but not in a bad way. But, for a while maybe I did worry it would make me less. And I want to apologize because I didn't really think of you as less. It just made you more…" Jay felt like a jerk. He was fucking this up and he really didn't mean it how the words may seem.

But Landon, bless him, smiled and chuckled lightly before pecking a kiss to Jay's lips. "I get it. You thought it made sense because I'm gay. And it made you *more* gay."

Jay shrugged and felt his cheeks heat. Landon hugged Jay tightly. "Jay, being with a man and wanting a relationship with a man made you not-so-straight. This is just another way to be together. It's not important that we do this. But I do love you so much for wanting to do it, to give me this."

"Thank you. And I do. I do want so much to give you this. That's why I even started with all this crazy talk."

Landon's expression grew naughty, but his gaze still held so much love, Jay's heart felt full to bursting. Landon ground his hard, naked cock into Jay's. Jay hissed in pleasure. "Anyone ever tell you you think too much?"

"Never," Jay said, seriously.

"Fair point. Well, it's not such a bad thing for me you do now. But *right now* let's turn off that brain of yours." Landon sucked in Jay's bottom lip, nibbling on it, using one of his strong, calloused hands to rub down Jay's flank then to his ass cheek, which he kneaded firmly.

Jay's heart thumped harder, cock tingled as Landon's slid next to it. Landon gave one last, long kiss before sitting back on his haunches and pushing Jay's legs up, directing Jay to hold them open wide, gripping under the knees. Landon grabbed one of the extra pillows beside Jay's head and maneouvered it under Jay's hips.

"I'll admit, I've never been with a virgin," Landon said, seemingly unsure. "I want this to be good for us. My first time was with someone who knew what they were doing and it still had its awkward moments, so I can't promise it won't hurt or be strange. But I'm going to do some stuff to try to make it less… all of that."

Jay could only nod as he looked down at Landon whose hand was running up and down one of Jay's inner thighs, while the other stroked Jay's cock. Even the tips of Jay's ears burned, feeling a bit embarrassed as Landon flicked his gaze from Jay's face to his hard cock to his exposed hole. Jay could definitely say this was new, and not wholly comfortable, but they naked yearning in Landon's eyes had Jay's cock rigid.

Without preamble, Landon bent and sucked Jay into his mouth. Jay grunted, canting his hips up a bit, getting a dirty laugh from Landon as he started bobbing his head up and down, sucking Jay's cock like a master. Jay's head lolled as he gave over to the feeling.

Landon started playing with Jay's balls, every once in a while stroking Jay's spit-slicked shaft. He pulled off, breathing loudly. "Damn Jay, you always taste so good."

Jay couldn't quite form words, but his cock jerked in Landon's hand so he figured that was response enough. Landon stroked Jay's wet cock, leaning up to kiss and nibble on each of Jay's nipples which had Jay bucking in Landon's hands. "Landon, damn. You're gonna make me lose it."

Landon stopped and pulled back a bit, eyes roaming over Jay. "You're so beautiful."

Jay flushed, this time with pride because the gleam in Landon's eyes, the way his licked his lips wantonly said even with Jay's forming lovehandles and his softer tummy, the man really did want him. The confidence that zapped through Jay, the capital-L love made him preen.

Landon spit on his hand, which made Jay laugh because it was crude as hell, but sexy in the strangest way, knowing what the man could do with that spit.

Landon rubbed the spit down Jay's perineum then the tip of his finger found Jay's sensitive opening and started rubbing circles around his hole. Jay instinctively pulled his legs wider, eyes bulging as he let out a moan.

"You like?" Landon's voice was husky and eager.

"It's different." Jay said, but pushed against the finger that played on his rim. Different but good, he wanted to say, but his voice failed him again as Landon spit and lubed his hole again. Then, as open as Jay'd felt earlier, the way he felt metaphorically undone by Landon, now became a physical openness as Landon slid the tip of a finger in.

"Breathe out," Landon said. Jay complied and Landon's thick finger slid in deep. Landon had been right earlier, when he said it'd hurt and feel awkward. Jay's erection flagged, but he couldn't stop the strange need to push down rather than retreat when Landon slowly started fingering him. Jay cried out when Landon inserted a second finger and crooked them, pressing something deep inside that made Jay shudder from head to heaven-pointed toes.

"Goddamn," Jay said through gritted teeth. His cock gave a happy jerk as Landon did it again, chuckling at Jay's reactions.

"I love how dirty your mouth gets in bed."

Jay only grunted in response. Landon pushed in a third finger after adding more spit. Jay watched Landon who stared heatedly at where his fingers entered Jay. He'd never been looked at like that by another person, like he was what they needed rather than just wanted.

Landon stroked Jay's cock, which had hardened again, even if not quite as hard as it had before. Which was strange because Jay felt like he had the most raging hardon he'd ever had. He really got what it meant to be completely turned on.

Landon pulled his fingers out. "Okay." Landon fitted himself between Jay's legs again, kissing Jay fully on the lips, then diving his tongue into Jay's mouth. Landon's tongue was cool from his having been breathing heavily through his mouth. Jay didn't understand why something so simple sent a thrill through him, but he'd learned at this point, everything about Landon, everything the man did was erotic to him.

"Okay," Landon repeated. "As much as I'd love to look in your eyes and be all cheesy and romantic this time, it's your first time, so it'll be easier this way." Landon removed the pillow from under Jay and positioned him on his side, one leg up slightly, then Landon spooned him from behind.

"Remember, breathe out," Landon whispered in Jay's ear.

Jay closed his eyes and did as he was told, the blunt head of Landon's cock prodding his hole. He wasn't freaking out, just overwhelmed. This was it. He'd realized when he and Landon were together what being one could really feel like, even if that was "cheesy"—as Landon put it. But this...

"Breathe," Landon whispered. Jay did. And holy shit. He gritted his teeth as Landon's long, thick cock slid inside him. Definitely bigger than two fingers, Jay felt split open.

"Keep breathing."

Jay realized then, he'd been holding his breath so he let it out and started breathing deeply. That definitely helped. Landon pushed all the way inside, then reached for Jay's cock, stroking him firmly, keeping him, hard with rough, dry, circular strokes over this head. Jay's body quaked, loosening. He tested the newfound muscles and willed them to open more. He didn't let his brain take over. This was about feeling. This was about him and Landon.

This was about being new.

Landon's mouth teased over Jay's shoulders and neck; he nibbled behind Jay's ear. Jay pushed back against Landon's invading cock.

"Oh yeah," Landon said, tone silly. "That means you're ready for the big show, baby."

Jay laughed on a moan as Landon slid out and then slowly back in. "Mother fucker," Jay groaned.

"Yeah? You like that?"

Boy, howdy. Landon used his own knee to push Jay's up some more, wrapped his arm around Jay's chest and set up a steady fucking. Jay eventually found himself fucking himself on Landon's cock. Landon stilled him though, placing a hand on Jay's lower belly, pushing slowly in, to the root.

"Let me love you," Landon said.

Jay couldn't even bring himself to laugh at the word. Now, he kinda got why people said things like that. He felt like a teenager who'd just realized you could love with your body as much as you could get off with it. And as Landon filled him, retreated, and filled him again. Jay felt so perfect, so cherished and so damned happy he'd run over here this morning, so glad he'd offered his body like this, because he did feel every bit of their bond like this. In Landon's arms, Jay's eyes started to leak, some from sadness for the man who'd been locked away all these years in his head, some from the happiness he'd found this when he'd not even known he'd needed it.

"Jay?" Landon stilled. "Babe, are you crying?"

"I'm fine," Jay said, choked. "Please. Keep going."

Landon stayed still another moment before kissing Jay's temple softly, reaching a hand down to fondle Jay's balls as he started thrusting in and out again.

Eventually, the need won over, again and they were slamming into one another, Jay practically shouting every time Landon hit that spot inside.

"Oh, fuck. Landon… I'm gonna cum."

"Do it!" Landon ground out into Jay's ear and both of them wrapped their hands around Jay's cock. Jay's vision blurred as he tipped over into the most intense orgasm he'd ever had. "Oh, son of a bitch," Landon barked out. Suddenly he was rolling Jay onto his stomach. Jay yelped happily as his sensitive cock thrust against the sheets and spurted more cum, his whole body convulsing. Landon hit that spot inside again and again as he flexed against Jay's ass, face buried in Jay's hair.

Then Landon pushed in deep, felt like he tried to crawl inside Jay as he shot his cum in Jay's ass and whimpered. Jay's heart pounded and he gripped Landon's hand that had wrapped around his chest, holding Landon as Landon emptied inside him. Jay wondered how he'd gone so long without this, never wanted to be without it again.

Being filled with Landon's cock, filled with his cum, Jay'd never felt so fucking close to someone before.

Landon pulled out, both of them letting out disappointed grunts as Jay's body released Landon's. Landon fell on the pillow next to Jay. "Jesus."

Jay rolled onto his back and caught his breath, reaching out a hand to lay on Landon's stomach. Landon grabbed it with one of his own and they lay in happy, sated silence for a while.

"That. Was. Awesome." Jay said around breaths.

Landon snorted. "Glad to be of service. So. Regular

part of our repertoire?"

"Maybe not so much." Jay twisted his hips, feeling the strange sensation, still full and aching in good and awkward ways. "How do you deal with all that… going on afterwards."

"It was your first time. It gets a little…. Okay, a lie. It's more intense your first couple times, but yeah. I know bottoming isn't for everyone."

Jay rolled over and looked at Landon, then kissed his forehead. When he leaned back up, the serene smile on Landon's face made his chest feel warm from the inside out. He felt like a little kid when he wrapped his arms around Landon, burrowing his head under Landon's chin, rolling on top of him. "Fuckin' A, Landon Petty. I love you!" He playfully hugged Landon tightly and Landon guffawed.

"You're ridiculous, Jay Hill." Landon wrapped his arms around Jay and squeezed him back, too tight. "But I love you too, you silly bastard."

Silly. Something he'd only ever called himself. But he couldn't say he'd ever been in better humor than he was today. He'd definitely never been so in love as he was today.

***

The next Monday at work, Landon walked in with not a little swagger. Ms Lynne scowled, but she'd been given what for by Landon's mama over her gossiping so whatever thoughts she had, she kept to herself. After Landon told his mama it wasn't idle gossip, she'd said "Well it wasn't her business to be spreading, anyway, then. It's a family matter."

Family. Landon had to admit, even with the personal red tape they still had to get through, Landon thought the word summed up what could be. Landon signed his mileage sheet, counting the days till he was finished with that particular task, then headed back to Jay's office.

They'd agreed to maintain as they had, be circumspect at work. They did still live in Montgomery County and the crew was still full of men who wouldn't appreciate Jay and Landon's type of love. But that didn't mean Landon had to ignore the man. After all, he hadn't seen him in two days. Silly or not, he'd missed Jay. But Jay's kids had needed him.

He knocked on the door and found his daddy sitting in one of the chairs across the desk from Jay.

"Oh, sorry, guys. I can come back later." Dammit.

Landon's daddy stood, heaving a sigh. "Naw. I'll get out y'all's way." The slight turning up of one side of his daddy's lips relieved some of the tension Landon hadn't realized was there. "No more neckin' in the office, though." His daddy pointed at Landon.

Landon and Jay both quailed.

Ricky belly laughed. Old bastard. "Y'all ain't very smooth." He grew somber. "But I don't want trouble for y'all. I suspect there will be some, anyway." His daddy looked at him. "Landon, I was just telling Jay here that I'm not okay with this. But I'm okay with this."

Landon's brows went up. His daddy rarely discussed his being gay. In fact, the statement was down right confusing. But he nodded, acknowledging his daddy was trying. That's more than most of the old timers around those parts would do.

"Figure y'all got enough trouble without me getting on your case. Just don't cause no troubles for us here, okay? You'll be done in a few months, then you two can… Do whatever you two do." Ricky looked decidedly uncomfortable with those words.

"Yessir," Landon and Jay said in unison. Their gazes met, Jay's held more than a little humor. Ricky harrumphed and made his way out.

"Well. That was something," Jay said.

"They've had a long while to get used to it. Remember, I told 'em years ago."

Jay nodded sagely. "I remember you'd said that. Guess after all the drama, I expected something more climactic."

"I think we've had enough of those climaxes." Landon fluttered his eyes at Jay. "I can think of other climaxes to focus on now."

Jay let out a put-upon sigh. "That's not keeping it out of the office."

"Gotta get it where I can," Landon teased. Jay shook his head, resigned but smiling.

"What do you need, Petty?"

"Just came to see how you were."

Jay leaned back in his chair and crossed his arms over his chest. "I'm good. Things at home are still tense with the girls."

Landon's eyes widened. "Beth's still here?"

"Oh, naw. She went back the other night after I left your house. But Millie has been spending a lot of time on the phone with her." Jay frowned. "She's probably gonna go live with her mama when she moves back here after Christmas."

"Oh, Jay," Landon said, moving to sit on Jay's desk, putting a hand out. He felt relief wash through him when Jay's frown morphed into a half-smile and he took Landon's hand, giving it a quick squeeze before letting it go. "It'll be okay. Probably would have turned out that way, either way, once Bethany moved back down. This is just sooner than I'd thought."

"You think it'll be okay."

Jay looked at Landon fondly. "I know it will."

"If you need anything..."

"I do," Jay responded.

"Oh?"

"The kids are going to their school's fall something-or-other tomorrow night. Curfew isn't til eight, so I need you to invite me over to yours. Maybe we'll have some dinner. Just the two of us."

Landon's cheeks hurt from smiling so much. "I'd like that." Landon looked toward the half-open office door then shot a smirk Jay's way. "Think you're too sore for us to give that a go again?"

Jay choked on the coffee he'd been drinking. "Damn you, Landon."

"That a no?"

Jay's cheeks turned that shade of pink Landon loved, more because it reminded him of how Jay flushed when his dick was in Landon's mouth than anything.

"We'll see," Jay said with dignity. "Now, go. I've got work to do."

Landon hopped off the desk and started to head out. Jay called to Landon, pulling him up short. He turned and the smile on Jay's face brilliantly lit the room, a man found. Life wasn't perfect, there was much to figure out but, hey, that smile was worth everything so far, and anything to come.

Epilogue

2 Years Later

Grumbling as he signed and filed his final grades, Landon missed simpler days of filling out mileage log sheets. Not that he'd go back to that, but Lord he was glad the school year was over and he had no more averages to figure or papers to grade.

He shut down his computer and left his classroom for the last time—well, for two months anyway. Checking his watch, he whistled happily when he noticed he still had an hour to make it home. Clint's graduation party was that night then he and Jay were off to the beach for two weeks.

They'd damn well earned the vacation.

Jay had hemmed and hawed about the trip, feeling bad for leaving his new job managing the office at a feed and seed co-op in a small town about fifteen miles from where they lived. The adjustment after people started catching on to their relationship a year earlier had led to Jay's not being able to function as supervisor at the saw mill. It'd never gotten too hostile, thankfully, but it'd been bad enough Landon's daddy had been more than willing to give a good reference when Jay'd found a new job.

He was closeted to his employees, there, mostly, but the owner was a lesbian so she was at least on his side. Landon hated how rough it'd been, but the pay was decent. Jay, though, felt so much loyalty to the woman who'd hired him that he'd not wanted to leave her in a lurch for two weeks.

But it was going to happen, dammit. They'd not gone further than a weekend Christmas shopping in Birmingham the previous holiday. They'd lived in their separate housed up until last week when Clint had graduated.

Granted, Clint had been easily won over in the end and had adjusted fairly well. Landon had figured it wouldn't be so bad, and he was right. Even Millie had come around in her own time. They were young enough, and had enough gay friends now, it didn't register as an issue.

But out of respect and Jay being cautious about anything to do with his kids so far as a step-parents went, they'd not forced the issue until they'd been together a little over a year. Landon didn't have much experience with dating, especially guys with kids, but he figured it had been par for the course. Even Bethany hadn't introduced her new boyfriend until they'd hit the six month mark a few months back.

Landon made it the few miles to their new house. The one they'd picked together, after they'd sold off their old houses. It was in Starkville. Not the most liberal town, but a college town and boasting more than twenty-thousand people, it felt like a safer bet than staying together in the country. Rome wasn't built in a day, and Montgomery County wouldn't be ready for gays in a hundred more years.

After turning off his truck, Landon made his way in the new house, a brick rancher just outside of town. He was happy to see Jay'd used the day off to finish emptying the boxed that'd been lying around the house.

The house may be a couple of thirty-something men, and neither was too good with decorating, but they could at least not look like hobos when they were having a party for Clint.

Millie came flying out of the kitchen, but stilled when she saw Landon. "Oh, sorry. Thought you were Clint."

She'd shot up like a weed lately, and even he couldn't believe how much older she looked at fourteen. He'd only been around the last couple of years, but he had grown attached to Jay's kids. Lord knows they were as close as he'd ever get to being a parent. And that was A-okay with Landon.

"No. He's not supposed to be here for another hour at least."

"Good. Dad is trying—and failing hard-core—to put together that surround sound y'all got. He wanted to use it for the music or something. Meanwhile, he hasn't put together any of the stuff for the party."

Landon winced. "Does he know what time it is?"

"Please," she said with a scoff. "You know how he gets when he's putting together stuff and not asking for help. He's been cussing and throwing things around in the den for an hour."

Landon sighed. "Great."

"The house looks nice, by the way." Millie's compliment was genuine, which made Landon smile goofily. He and Jay both worried how the kids would take it with them actually co-habitating. It'd possibly held Landon up more than Jay until papers were signed and it was all over but the moving.

"You're cool, right?" He asked.

"For the millionth time, yes." She shook her head, exasperated, and looked so much like her dad it hurt. Landon wanted to hug her, but he still didn't have his footing where that stuff was concerned, she he just patted her shoulder. He heard Jay saying in his head *"You'll get it in time."*

"Is your mom coming?"

Millie grimaced. "Um. Not so much. She did a dinner for him with my grandparents last night. I don't think Clint wanted to tell dad, though, in case it hurt his feelings."

Landon sighed. Yeah, Bethany still wasn't on Team Hill-Petty. She wasn't cruel, and she still spoke with Jay frequently. She even bought Landon a Christmas gift. But awkward was definitely the appropriate way to describe her continued reaction to anything that involved Jay and Landon as a unit. He wasn't all that surprised she wouldn't be coming over to their new home for a while. He hoped for Jay and the kids' sake, though, she'd come sooner rather than later.

"Well, let me go tell your dad and get his butt in gear. Will you go get the table cloths on the picnic tables out back?"

She gave a nod and shot out to the garage, where they'd put all decorations.

Landon walked into the den, which was a separate room from the living room. The sunken in space was one of the features that'd made them jump on this particular house. Watching football had brought them together and still remained one of their favorite activities together, so a man-cave had been a dream when they'd looked around for a house.

Landon chuckled to himself when he saw Jay bent over behind the catty-corner flat screen TV, wires draped over his shoulders.

"Jay. Could you have picked a worse day to do this?" Landon smirked at his boyfriend. God he loved that word as it related to Jay, even if it sounded juvenile to some.

Jay straightened and scowled at Landon. "Damn."

"What?"

"Dad, really? This was *your* idea."

Landon turned to see Clint and Millie looking exasperated and fairly amused.

"I know. I just didn't know it'd be so complicated."

"We need to set up for *me* now, so wing it."

Jay scowled at his son, who walked over and shoved papers in his hands. "Come on, Millie. This could be a while."

"God, and they might start kissing." Millie gave a mock shudder. Landon didn't get offended. She meant that as a teenager who had to witness their parents kissing, nothing else. They'd both seen Jay and Landon be affectionate at that point.

"Well. Damn."

"You said that already," Landon said.

Jay came from behind the TV, dropping wires and cables. "Damn."

Landon huffed.

"Sorry. I just.. last time I did this someone was pregnant so I thought I'd go for romance."

Landon's heart stopped. Jay shuffled from foot to foot. "Jay?"

"So, since we're leaving tomorrow, I wanted to talk about this today, since you were done with school and we could celebrate and it could be a honeymoon. I didn't think about having a house full of teenagers and your parents."

Landon knew his jaw was dropped but he couldn't shut his mouth. He also couldn't help Jay out because… Hell, he'd been so happy they were living together, still hadn't thought of marriage as an option—not in the south. Of course he wanted to be married one day, he'd dreamed, but until just the last while it hadn't been possible where they lived and as much as Landon wanted marriage, he didn't think he wanted to move that far from his roots to make it happen.

And as Jay shuffled nervously, Landon realized if Jay proposed, there wouldn't be some commitment ceremony with vows just in front of their friends and tons of paperwork with an attorney. They could…

"I didn't know what the hell I was doing the first time I got married. Then I didn't know what the hell I was doing when we divorced. I sure as hell didn't know what I was doing when you and I got together or started being more to each other. I didn't know what I was doing when it clicked in my head that I wanted this forever." Jay stopped shuffling, took a deep breath and that same determination returned, the kind he'd had when he'd raced to Landon's house two years ago to tell Landon he loved him. Landon saw it in his eyes and it choked him up.

"The last couple of years with you has been scary, and sometimes stressful, and I've had too much damn self-evaluation and my brain's been all crazy. But you have always stood by me, been my rock, been the person who made me smile, made it alright."

Jay walked up to Landon. "I didn't think you'd appreciate flowers or a diamond. You're a simple guy, like me. We have the same roots and come from the same place. That's another thing I love about you and you say you love about me. So I hope, this simple moment where this simple man hands you these papers, that thank God, only need a simple signature nowadays is enough to show you I never ever want to be without you again."

Landon looked at the papers Jay'd handed to him. The application for a marriage license in the county they'd be vacationing in. "How'd—"

"Oh, those kids and their Google. They got 'em." Jay watched Landon expectantly. "Uh, I hate to rush you, but we have no time til—"

Landon jumped at Jay, hugging him. "You fucking silly bastard." Landon hugged Jay tight, not wanting to let go. "And we can, can't we?" Landon could hear the awe in his own voice, realizing even in their town in Missi-fucking-ssippi, they'd be for real married. He'd be married to Jay Hill.

"What d'you think? Former heterosexual worth the risk?"

Landon kissed Jay's lips, then laughed and kissed his chin and his eyelids and his cheeks. "Fuck yes. So much yes."

Jay seemed to sag with that and they embraced. Then Jay pulled back with an "Oh, yeah." He dug into his pocket and pulled out a simple gold band. Landon blinked, trying not to get too emotional, but failing as he realized just how fucking significant the ring Jay held was.

"Look inside."

Landon cocked his head as he took the band from Jay and read the inside inscription.

Borrowed trouble. Worth it. Landon tossed his head back and laughed. "You're ridiculous."

Jay took Landon's hand. "Let's go help the kids."

"And you're terrible romantic," Landon said, drily. Then he stopped Jay, tugging his hand. "Wait. What were you doing with the TV?"

"It was a recording of the first football game we ever watched at Woody's."

Landon snorted.

"What? That's romantic!" Jay sniffed, offended.

"Romantic is letting me do what I wanted to do when Felicia was flirting with you that night?"

"Why would I let you punch me?"

Landon shoved Jay's shoulder, playfully, then put his face next to Jay's ear. "I wanted to fuck you over that bar. I didn't want anyone's hands on you but mine."

Jay cleared his throat and they both looked over to the wet bar they'd installed in the den before they moved in.

"You just had to say shit like that while the kids are here," Jay grumbled.

"The beautiful part is…" Landon kissed Jay one

more time. "That'll be here a long time. And so will we. A long, long time. Together."

Jay's face went soft and happy. "Yeah. We will."

THE END

About the Author

Kade Boehme is a southern boy without the charm, but all the sass. Currently residing in New York City, he lives off of ramen noodles and too much booze.

He is the epitomy of dorkdom, only watching TV when Rachel Maddow or one of his sports teams is on. Most of his free time is spent dancing, arguing politics or with his nose in a book. He is also a hardcore Britney Spears fangirl and has an addiction to glitter.

It was after writing a short story about boys who loved each other for a less than reputable adult website that he found his true calling, and hopefully a bit more class. A member of Romance Writers of America's New York City Chapter and Rainbow Writers of America, Kade works as a full time writer.

He hopes to write about all the romance that he personally finds himself allergic to but that others can fall in love with. He maintains that life is real and the stories should be, as well.

He loves to hear from readers, so feel free to get in touch with Kade:

Twitter: https://twitter.com/kaderadenurface
Facebook: http://facebook.com/kade.adam
Blog: http://kaderade.blogspot.com/
E-mail: kadeboehmewrites@gmail.com

MORE BOOKS BY THIS AUTHOR

Novellas

*Wide Awake**

You Can Still See the Stars in Seattle (Wide Awake #2)

*A Little Complicated**

*Gangster Country**

Wood, Screws, & Nails with Piper Vaughn

*Keep Swimming**

*Going Under (Keep Swimming #2)**

*Chasing the Rainbow**

Novels

*Don't Trust the Cut**

*Trouble & the Wallflower**

*Where the World Ends**

Teaching Professor Grayson with Allison Cassatta *

We Found Love with Allison Cassatta*

*Chance of the Heart**

SHORT STORIES

Proud Heart: A Chance & Bradley Pride Short

*available in paperback

9 781517 799656